Double Wedding Ring

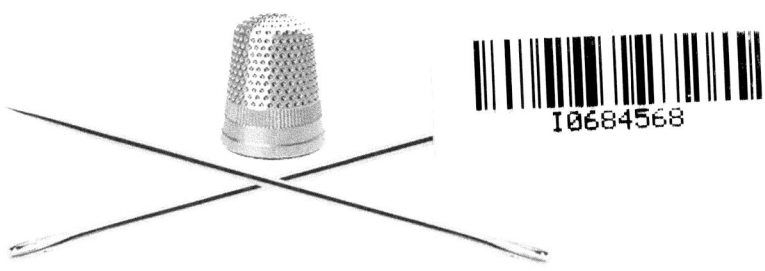

Final Volume of
The Guild in the Granary Trilogy

by

Lynn Thompson

The Trilogy
The Guild in the Granary
Timeless Star
Double Wedding Ring

ISBN 978-0692707050

Dedication

This book is dedicated to the members of the Grove City Writer's Group who have dragged me whining and crying to the end of this book before I could allow myself to move on to a different one.

Thanks to Janet Shailer, Rosemary Barkas, Liz Thompson, Barbara Whittington, Susan Brunner and everybody else.

DOUBLE WEDDING RING

Chapter 1

Caroline Clarkson's life was a mess. Her husband Charles had left her in the middle of some mid-life miasma neither of them understood. He had just announced one evening that he was tired of being married and wanted a break. Her two daughters, Jamie and Budd were leaving the nest and befouling it on the way out. Jamie was living in sin with some want-to-be lawyer in Bowling Green, Ohio and Budd was spending way too much time with a boy who attended Ohio State while she was still in high school. Caroline's business, a quilt shop called Always in Stitches, was losing money on a weekly basis. Her financial situation was dire. She might even have to close the shop.

Her life was out of control. She wondered what more could go wrong. She wanted to return to the days when Charles loved her and they both knew it; the days when the girls were young and thought she knew everything. These days, she lay in bed mornings, afraid to get up and greet the day less something else tragic happened. The empty king-sized bed she had shared with Charles for years felt as big as a football field . She was in that bed Tuesday morning when the phone rang. Nan, her shop assistant, was on the other end.

"Caroline, a quilting bus is outside waiting for me to unlock the door. Were we expecting a tour bus this morning?" Nan's voice was energetic but filled with uncertainty.

Caroline sat up, wiped a hand across her face. "No, I don't know anything about a tour bus. Kathy's scheduled to work this morning. Is she there?"

"I haven't seen or heard from her," Nan said. "The women are looking through the glass door. They can see I'm in here. They're starting to bang on the door. What should I do?"

"Unlock the door, Nan, and smile. I'll be there as soon as I can." Caroline clicked the phone off and rolled over. Charles' side of the bed was undisturbed. She got perverse pleasure from stirring up his covers before she arose. It allowed her to release some of the discontent that had taken residence in her heart. She tugged and pulled the blanket and sheets till they looked used. She rolled around making a mess of them. Only then did she slowly rise up from her lonely bed. She hadn't the time or inclination for a shower so she dragged a comb through her graying blond hair and pulled on a pair of sweat pants she'd left on the floor the night before. She managed to find a tee shirt in the basket of clean laundry she had carried upstairs last night. It was only a little wrinkled; she pulled it over her head.

Before she left the bedroom she squirted herself liberally with Sarah Jessica Parker's Lovely perfume. Charles gave it to her on her last birthday. On the one hand she missed Charles after twenty-three years of marriage and many good days together. She hated missing Charles. She wanted him to come home but she'd never let him know. He was angry about something when he left but she wasn't sure what. She wondered if even Charles knew. They had allowed themselves to leak into a separation. Caroline loved Charles, she had always loved Charles, but the romance was definitely gone from the marriage. It was sad. She yearned for predictability, she longed for someone besides herself to carry the laundry basket upstairs. She wanted a partner for the rest of her life, but she wasn't sure it should be Charles.

Carolyn blinked at the mess in the kitchen as she passed through to the garage. It was chilly even for an early

September morning. From the garage coat rack, she grabbed a light jacket that in a former life had belonged to one of her daughters. She shouldered into it. The Buick started after only two tries and she backed out into the street. She and Charles had lived at 2908 since the girls were babies. It used to be a happy place filled with love and laughter. A place where you knew what was going to happen next. Now it was a sad house where she and Budd rattled around like peas. She thought even Budd was ignoring her since Charles left. They'd both have to move if Charles didn't come home. She thought about the dreadful prospect of moving while she drove to the quilt shop.

The bus was a double-decker luxury cruiser. It was almost blocking the entrance to the parking area behind Always in Stitches. Caroline slowed down to squeeze through the narrow space the driver had left her and anybody else wanting to get into the parking area. The driver was leaning against the back wall of the building with a half-smoked cigarette dangling from his lips. There were three butts on the ground. The driver was wearing a backward facing ball cap. Unkempt salt and pepper hair peeked out around the edges of the cap. He had matching salt and pepper stubble on his chin.

"We weren't expecting a bus tour this morning," Caroline said.

The drive shrugged. "The ladies wanted to stop. They insisted when we drove by. I had to go around the block and come back," he said. "It will throw off the schedule for the whole day." He shrugged again. "I get paid by the hour."

Caroline gave him a scowl and walked into the shop. Nan was frantically ringing up sales for a line of ladies who were laughing and spending money like only a bunch of partying quilters can. Nan's hair was pulled back into a pair of pony tails on either side of her head. She looked like a four-year-old. The register was working hard as Nan rang up sales. This should have boosted Caroline's spirits, but it didn't. It would help her sagging bottom line. She did pitch in, offering help, cutting fabric and doing her best to smile. By the time the last sale was rung and the final trio of women returned to the bus, Kathy arrived with excuses and apologies for being late. Kathy was late often enough that Caroline had heard it all before.

Nan brushed escaped hair back from her forehead and smiled, "It was exciting there for a minute. Let's see how we did?" She pushed the cash register button that showed total sales. "$2,145," she said. "More than half of last week's total already this morning." She clapped her hands gleefully.

Most of the fabric was put way when a tooth-chattering roar came from the floor. It was Robert Arven, downstairs, in the small engine repair shop. He'd forgotten to take his work into the sound proof room. Caroline stomped her foot on the floor until it hurt. In five seconds another bang came. It was a broom handle banging against the ceiling. Robert wouldn't forget the sound proofing again, at least not again today.

This was the communication system Caroline and Robert had worked out when Schultz, the landlord, rented the shop downstairs to Robert's small engine repair business. Caroline thought it had been a dreadful decision for the building which was an old granary and for Always in Stitches in particular because it dealt in fine cotton fabrics that had nothing in common with the oily residue the motor people tracked through the shop when they took a wrong turn. On one of Robert's first visits to the quilt shop, he had ended up buying several yards of nice cotton fabrics that he accidentally touched. He was still using the fabric as shop rags. The best shop rags in town, he said.

Robert and Caroline were trying to make the best of a bad situation. Some days it worked. Some days, it didn't

Chapter 2

The women were still working to restore order to the shop at mid-morning when Aggie McDaniel came in. Aggie was a regular volunteer and was in the shop today to help cut scarlet and grey table runners. You could sell a scarlet and grey Edsel in central Ohio, if you had one. The Ohio State University was located nearby and anything in the school colors of scarlet and gray sold.

Aggie was the current president of the quilting guild that met in the granary. She was in her eighties and had the wisdom of a lady her age and a steely sense of what was right and what was wrong. In spite of that, her silhouette was soft and fluffy like a down pillow and her hair was controlled in a grey bun. Today she had the bun decorated with a red scarf.

Quilting brought women of all ages together just like it had done since thread was invented.. The three women worked in harmony. Caroline and Nan cutting table runner pieces; Aggie folded the pieces and put them into plastic bags along with instructions. They had a nice rhythm going.

The bells on the back door tinkled and Michael Lomand's bulk blocked the light. Michael was a chef, owned his own restaurant, and combed flea markets, garage sales and e-bay searching for antique quilts and needlework. His restaurant was called Michael's Restaurant in big letters "Cajun specialties" in smaller letters. He carried his tiny powder puff of a dog, Della, in a pet container in one hand and a brown paper bag in the other.

"Michael, I wasn't expecting to see you today," Caroline said.

"Wait till you see what I've found," he said.

He lay the brown paper bag on the cutting table and pulled out a quilt. The quilt was wrapped in tissue paper. Michael pulled on a pair of white cotton gloves and handed a second pair to Caroline. The quilt was a double wedding ring pattern in faded shades of coral, red, ecru and green with a white background. It was hand stitched and quilted with fine needlework.

"Look at this," Michael said. He showed Caroline the inscription on the lower, back corner of the quilt. Marietta Harper 1876.

"Wow," Aggie said. "Can I use the gloves?" she asked Caroline who peeled them off and handed them over to her.

Aggie "oohed" and "aahed" over Michael's quilt. "This is a very old quilt. Did it cost you a fortune?"

"I found it in a box of linens in a sale by the side of the road in southern Ohio. A pair of brother's were selling off the goods from their mother's house. They had no idea what they were selling. I offered them twenty dollars for the entire box and they were happy to take it."

Aggie's mouth dropped open and her eyes got wide. "You're kidding?"

"Can you imagine picking up a bargain like that by the side of the road?" Caroline asked.

"I think he makes more money collecting quilts than he does owning a restaurant," Aggie said. "Still a good thing it was sons who were cleaning out the house. A woman would have had a clue about the value of this quilt."

"You're probably right, Aggie," Michael said. "Double wedding ring quilts are dated from about 1929 according to quilt historians. But this one has a nineteenth century date worked right into it. It could be quite a significant find, worth a few thousand dollars. It's going to take some research to figure out what we actually have here"

Aggie and Michael continued to examine the quilt while their heads bobbed together over it. "Will you bring the quilt to the guild meeting next week?" Aggie asked.

"I will," Michael said. "I want to share this great find with the rest of the ladies." The two folded up the quilt and put it back in the brown paper bag. "I'm going to take the quilt to the Historical Society this afternoon and see what I can learn."

"Good Luck," Aggie said. "We'll hope for a full report at the guild meeting next week."

"I'm pretty excited myself," Michael said. "Wouldn't it be something if we could verify the double wedding ring design was made during the civil war."

"It would be the first one," Caroline said.

"Really?" Nan asked.

"It was featured in a Caper's Weekly magazine in 1929. Surely the pattern must have existed before it landed in the magazine."

"I will let you know what I find out," Michael said. Little Della whined from her cage. "She's been in the cage a while. I need to take her outside for a break."

Aggie nodded. "I love solving these mysteries. Go, Michael, go."

Michael collected the dog, the quilt and left the shop.

Chapter 3

The women fell silent again and continued to cut fabric and stuff bags. The silence and the rhythm of the work gave the shop a cozy ambiance.

It was interrupted when three women came in the front door. Two of them were wearing identical long homespun dresses reminiscent of some long gone days. The third woman wore a powder blue cowgirl suit with lots of fringe and a matching pale blue cowgirl hat. They would have stood out in any crowd.

The ladies fingered fabric as they worked their way toward Caroline and the work table in the back of the shop. "Busy today, "Caroline said quietly to Aggie and Nan.

"Finally," Nan said.

"Can I help you?" Caroline asked moving up the aisle toward the women.

"We're from the Civil War Encampment out on Orders Road," the younger looking woman said.

"We've run out of quilting fabric," the other woman said, "And we have three more weeks before we move on to our final location of the season."

"Our fabric is all 100% cotton," Caroline said. She smiled at the three. "You wouldn't want anything else for a quality quilt."

The woman in the cowgirl suit stuck out her hand, "Hi, I'm alias Annie Oakley," she said. "I don't quilt but I do sharp-shooting demonstrations just like the real Annie Oakley."

Caroline took her hand and shook it."I wondered," she said nodding toward the woman's costume.

"How do you like it?" Annie said. "I buy the gloves and the hats but I make the shirts and skirts myself." She twirled in front of the other women. She wasn't embarrassed or shy about it at all. Everything was fringed; the bottom of her skirt, the gloves, the rim of her hat, the sleeves on her shirt. She was a sight.

"I like the color," Nan said.

"It picks up every bit of dust and soil," Annie said. "I have to wash it every time I wear it, but I like the pastels. I have the same suit in pink, lime, ecru and yellow." She brushed a bit of dust off her skirt.

Caroline turned to the other two women. "Can I cut something for you?"

"Do you have any civil war reproduction fabrics?" the younger looking woman asked.

"An entire section. Up the steps and to the left." Caroline said. "We have a lot of reproduction quilters who visit the shop. We try to keep a large variety of the fabrics they love."

"We don't use anything else. All of our quilts are civil war reproductions. You cannot find the fabric everywhere."

They piled up several bolts of fabric. "Three-quarters of a yard of each," said the older-looking woman. She patted the stack of bolts on the table. Nan took three of them to another table and began to cut. Caroline pushed aside the table runner pieces and Aggie began handing her bolts of fabric to cut.

"We're twins," the younger woman said. "My name is Melissa and that," – she pointed to her sister-," is Clarissa." Clarissa smiled at Caroline and the resemblance became more obvious.

Melissa said, "I color my hair and my sister refuses. That's why she looks so much older. I think it makes a huge difference." Melissa fingered a bag of table runner pieces. "You sell kits?" she asked.

"Yes," Caroline said.

Clarissa gave her sister a snotty look.

Caroline checked out the hair color difference between the twins and wondered what sort of a sister relationship would cause this topic to come up in such a casual situation.

"I HAVE A HUSBAND," Melissa said. "My sister is a widow and in serious need of a man. I'm just trying to help."

This seemed like an even more out-of-line comment. Caroline smiled, not knowing what to say. She suspected this was not the first time the women had had this very conversation and she sure didn't want to get into the middle of it. She did wonder if she'd be like Clarissa if Charles decided not to come home. It was a depressing prospect.

"You should come out to the encampment," Annie said. "And see what the quilting display has to offer."

"Yes," said Melissa. "You might even sell some of your kits."

Clarissa nodded.

"Who would I sell to out there?" Caroline asked.

"School children," Melissa said. "We have hundreds of them. They come and we teach them the basics of quilting. The little girls love it. The little boys, not so much. The boys like spending their time in the blacksmith shop."

"Maybe we should check it out," Nan said. She had her fabrics cut and carried them to the register.

"I'll think about it," Caroline said. "We have pot holder kits left over from the last girl scout group we had in here. They would be perfect to sell to kids." She took her fabric cuts to the register and Nan rang up the sale. Annie and Clarissa bickered over the bill. Clarissa ended up paying but there was friction between the women. Caroline thought they just didn't like one another for some reason.

The women exchanged good-byes and Caroline told the shoppers they might drive out to the encampment that afternoon if business didn't pick-up.

Chapter 4

Business did not pick up at Always in Stitches.

The encampment was two miles from town. Dust drifted up from the parking area as Nan and Caroline pulled in. They had left Aggie and Kathy at the shop to look after business. The parking area was half-full of cars. Two school busses were parked at the far end. The bus drivers stood in the shade of the busses, chatting. Nine and ten-year-old children ran from building to building in the village area of the encampment. Half the kids wore school uniforms, half didn't. All of them were kicking up dust and being noisy. The girls were holding hands and the boys were jostling and shoving one another. Some things never change..

"This is extremely cool," Nan said. "I wonder if Jack has seen it?" Her face was filled with tenderness whenever she spoke about Jack. She might become the boy's step-mother if things worked out between her and his dad.

Several tents were set up around the permanent buildings in the village. The tents were rag-tag like real civil war tents might be. Fire pits were flaming and smoking outside the tents. One woman was cooking bacon and eggs in an iron skillet. The smell of the bacon mixed with the smoke and the open air appealed to Caroline's genetic memory and took her back to a time before she was born. She could see the blacksmith shop, a general store and a school building.

They were widely spaced and filled with children. People in period costume and civil war uniforms hurried from one place to another. Nan's head swiveled as they walked between the tents. Beds were neatly rolled up and stashed out of the way. Campers smiled at the women as they passed. Small groups were gathered around several displays including axe throwing, firearms, and primitive musical instruments. Children stood by attentively as the re-enactors explained details of life in a civil war camp. It could have been 1864.

"We're looking for the quilting tent," Caroline said to a lady standing next to a medical display. The instruments looked like things you might find in the bottom of a tool box; corkscrews, pliers, metal rods and a rusty-looking saw. Caroline shuddered at the thought of the damage these things could do to the human body.

"Over that way," the woman said, pointing towards a tent full of goods that appeared to be for sale. The goods were laid out on tables and arranged in an orderly fashion.

"Thanks," Caroline said and the two women changed their direction. The first tent was filled with merchandise meant for sale; hats, bows and arrows, pretend tomahawks and books, lots of books. The proprietor was standing at the front of the tent rocking back and forth on the heels of his boots.

"Morning ladies," he said with a big smile. "Can I interest you in some of my wares?" The man was tall with long gray hair; quite good looking in a rough sort of way. He was wearing fringed pants, a plaid shirt and a grey felt hat. Caroline slowed down and took a second look. The man's eyes met hers. They were liquid gray and quite arresting. She couldn't help but smile back at him.

"No thanks," Nan said. "We're looking for the quilting tent."

The man reached out to Caroline and was shaking her hand. ""I'm Kenny," he said. Caroline lowered her eyes.

"We're looking for Melissa and Clarissa," Nan said.

"Ah, the quilting twins," Kenny said. "Quite a pair, aren't they?" His eyes never left Caroline's. He lifted her hand to his lips and kissed it. She didn't quite jerk it back, but almost.

Now that's something that doesn't happen every day. Caroline wasn't sure a stranger had ever kissed her hand before. Nan looked back and forth between the two. Their eyes were still locked. Caroline was clearly smitten. "The quilting tent," Nan said pointedly to Caroline.

"Yes, yes," she said.

Kenny released Caroline's hand. "That way." He pointed to the left.

"I see it," Nan said. She started toward the tent and Caroline followed. She was rubbing the hand Kenny had kissed against her cheek. "Wow," she said. "Wow. That man kissed my hand. But I'm a married woman. At least I think I am." She looked back over her shoulder at the man and he waved a small wiggly fingered wave.

The quilting tent was a large affair. Both sides of the tent door had the flaps pulled back and Nan and Caroline could see women seated around a quilting frame. It was set up in the middle of the tent and was clearly the center of attention. Small heads, and a few grown ones were bent over the quilt. Needles were going in and out of an Ohio Star quilt. Melissa and Clarissa were cutting quilt pieces at a table in the back of the tent. They were talking earnestly. Caroline recognized the fabric from her shelves.

Melissa saw Nan and Caroline. She started toward them and snagged the trim lady supervising the quilters by the arm as she came. "Shelah," she said. "These are the women from the quilt shop. I told you about them. Nan and Caroline, right?"

"Right," Caroline said.

"Shelah is our resident quilt expert," Melissa said. "She knows almost everything about civil war fabrics and the patterns used by civil war quilters. We're very proud of her."

"Really? Maybe we could have her speak to our quilt guild. One of our members brought in a quilt this morning. We think it dates from 1876."

"She does do speaking engagements and she's even working on a book about civil war quilts and fabrics," Clarissa said boldly. Her sister was right, she could take ten years off her appearance if she did something with her hair. It was a muddy gray and flying off in all directions like she'd stuck her finger in a light socket.

"We'll try to work something out. Our guild president is helping out in the shop today."

Shelah nodded. "I'd like that. We only have two more weeks here, then we move to our last location of the summer season. It would have to be soon. I'd like to see the quilt your guild member has found. Not many authentic civil war quilts still surviving."

"Caroline is thinking of bringing some kits out to sell to the beginning quilters. Pot holders and aprons. Right for the young sewer's skill levels," Melissa said.

"That would be a nice addition to our display," Shelah said. She pointed to one of the front corners by the open tent flaps. "Here," she said as she walked to the corner. "We can set up a card table and keep a few items on the table. You'd have to take care of your own money and bagging materials."

The ladies were discussing the details of the arrangement when Annie Oakley hurried up to them. "Are you joining us?" she asked. "My station is in the blacksmith's shop. You must come to see it. I do my demonstrations behind the shop at noon and at five o'clock. The area has to be cleared so I only get to do it twice a day. Clearly she was excited to see them and wanted to share her participation in the encampment activities.

Melissa was just as determined to maintain center stage and complete the arrangements. "On nice days you could set the table up in front of the tent," she said. "The children would like that."

"Good idea," Shelah said with exaggerated politeness. She took Annie's arm and pulled her into a warm hug. "I know the ladies will want to see your demonstration, Annie, but first we need to figure out what they are going to do here."

Annie nodded and stepped back. She had been chastened by Shelah, but with kindness.

"And what would it cost to set up a table?" Caroline asked.

"Nothing," Shelah said. "We're part of the educational program and don't have to pay a thing to be here. Everybody is a volunteer. You'd be under our little umbrella." Shelah smiled showing a gleaming set of teeth. "It would help you and it would help us."

"What do you think, Nan?"

Nan shrugged. Annie was shifting from foot to foot.

Melissa spoke again. "There's a hired security company that looks after the encampment at night. Most of the soldiers and families spend the nights in their tents. No worries."

"Nope, no worries," Annie said.

"Don't forget I'm taking some time off when Stan gets home," Nan said to Caroline.

"Yes, I remember. Still I think we should do it," Caroline said. "It can't do any harm to our bottom line, which needs help in the worst way right now. We'll take care of the schedule."

"Ha!" Shelah said. "When do you want to start?"

"Tomorrow. We'll need a bit of time to cut some small kits. We'll aim them toward the sewing skill of eight-year-olds and up." Shelah could almost see Caroline's brain working. She had risen to meet a challenge she could control. And she really could use the money to help out her bottom line. Hitting the proverbial two birds with one stone.

"What time should we be here?"

"Ten," Shelah said. "The children begin to arrive about 10:30 and leave by 2:00pm. The group is small today, only two busloads. Usually we have twice as many." She smiled at Caroline, "and I'm eager to hear more about coming to your guild meeting." Shelah walked back to the quilting frame where a girl was holding her hand in the air waiting for help.

"We're relying on you," Melissa said before she returned to the cutting table. Clarissa raised a hand in a wave.

"We'll be here." Caroline said.

Annie left with them, heading back to the blacksmith's shop. "You're going to love being here," she said. "A bunch of really nice people." Then she peeled away from Nan and Caroline toward the blacksmith shop. She hugged the tall, amiable salesman and then swooped back to Nan and Carline.

"Kenny," she said by way of explanation. "He's a really nice guy and sort of my boyfriend."

"Oh, how nice," Nan said. "We met him when we came in."

"Very friendly," Caroline said.

"He sort of looks after the single ladies at the encampment," Annie said.

Nan and Caroline smiled, not knowing what else to do.

Inside the blacksmith shop they looked over the Annie Oakley display and congratulated Annie on its historic value. She shared brochures about the real Annie Oakley's life and tips on sharp shooting. "Sorry we can't stay for the demonstration," Caroline said.

"You'll see it another day," Annie said. "I'm so happy you're going to be here with us. It does get boring as the season wears on and we are about to go home for the winter."

"When do you shut down for the winter?" Caroline asked.

"We have one more encampment before we finish our season," Annie said. "It's over near Dayton and we'll all do other things till the show starts up again in the spring."

"It's quite a commitment," Nan said.

"It is," Annie said. "We sort of get to be a family after a few weeks, except for the folks who join us regulars at each stop."

"Not everybody travels with you for the summer?"

"We pick up local re-enactors at every stop. Some stick with us for a few weeks or even a few days. Whatever time they have available."

"I had no idea," Nan said. "Thank you for doing this for all the people you see in a season."

Annie smiled. "It's very rewarding," she said. "I love the kids. A lot of them think I'm the REAL Annie Oakley they read about. I love that."

"You mean you're not," Caroline said and all three women laughed as they parted ways.

Nan and Caroline had to walk past Kenny's tent to get back to their car. "Hey ladies," he called out. "Come in, look around, buy something." He was shouting over the heads of a bunch of rowdy eight-year-old boys, who were checking out the wooden pop guns.

"We'll be back," Caroline said. "We'll look then. I may even buy one of your hats." Kenny made his way through the children so that he was close to Caroline. He took the hat off his head and placed it on hers. He stepped back, made a frame with his fingers, looked through the frame at Caroline. "It looks good," he said.

Caroline could feel the sweat around the band of the hat. It was warm and it was wet. She removed the hat, reached up and put it back on his head. She grabbed Nan by the arm and pulled her off toward the car before he could get his hands on her again.

"That guy is really flirting with you, "Nan said.

"And not very subtle about it either. The problem is; I like it."

Chapter 5

Back at the shop everyone got busy making pot holder kits and apron kits that would be appropriate for little girls. Caroline told Aggie about Shelah and the program she was willing to put on for the guild.

"That would be wonderful," Aggie said. "Michael has taken an interest in civil war quilts. I think he's working on a signature quilt right now. And of course he can bring in his new quilt for Shelah's assessment."

"He told me at the meeting last month that signature quilts were very popular during and before the civil war era. Women going west took along blocks signed by friends they were leaving behind and by women they met on their journey. It was a way to stay in touch." Aggie stuffed the pieces for a pot holder into a plastic bag.

"He's decided food service jobs are sort of similar with folks coming and going the way they do. He's gathered signature squares from several workers and even searched out a few from his past." She stuffed another bag. "I think he's having fun with it."

"Sounds like it," Caroline said.

"We should have Shelah come to our meeting next week. Especially since the encampment will be moving on in just two weeks."

"I'll let her know tomorrow," Caroline said.

Aggie eventually left to go to lunch with a friend and Goldie wandered through on her way to open the manicure/palm reader's studio where she worked four days a week. She had her hair pulled back with a bright blue and green turban tied around it. Her hair was still growing back after chemo treatments for breast cancer.

"What's up?" Goldie asked.

"We're setting up a sales booth at the civil war encampment out on Orders Road," Nan said. "It will be so much fun. Caroline already has a boyfriend."

Goldie raised her eyebrows and said, "Maybe I can go along and read some palms."

"Can you read the palms of children?" Caroline said.

"Of course you can," Goldie said. "The readings aren't perfectly accurate."

"Are any of them?" Kathy asked.

Goldie gave her a withering look. "You know they are. Look at how accurate I've been with Robert's readings."

Robert Arven and Goldie had become an item since Robert moved into the building. She gave him manicures like he was her only patron and bragged that he had the best looking hands of any mechanic in the city. She was right. She also read his palm which had facilitated a romance between the two of them.

Kathy shrugged and stacked packages of kits into the suitcase on wheels Caroline was using to transport them to the encampment.

"I've got to go open the manicure studio," Goldie said. "I have an appointment at 2."

"Are you just coming in for appointments these days?" Nan asked.

"Just today," Goldie said. "I had things to do at home this morning and Robert is taking me to supper after work this evening." Goldie winked at Caroline and wiggled her shoulders seductively. Then she walked out the door.

Nan and Caroline smiled at one another. "She sure has a way with the men, doesn't she," Nan said.

"Especially with Robert." Kathy shook her head and added the change box to the suitcase she was packing.

The phone rang and Nan reached over to answer it. "Hello". Silence. She smiled and looked up at Caroline. "It's Jamie," she mouthed. Jamie was Caroline and Charles's older daughter, a senior this year at Bowling Green in northern Ohio. Most of Caroline's profits from Always in Stitches went to pay Jamie's tuition. It had been a long financial haul and Caroline was grateful it was almost over.

Caroline reached for the phone and Nan turned away from her to prevent her taking it. Nan laughed into the phone and said, "Yes, it's been a good day. We had a tour bus in this morning and the women spent like there was no tomorrow." She listened again for a moment, said "Here's your mom," and then handed the phone to Caroline.

"Hi, Mom," Jamie said. "Glad you're having a good day." She was silent for several long beats. Without small talk or warming her mother up, she went right into the reason for her call. "Ted and I have a huge favor to ask."

"What else is new," Caroline said into the phone.

Jamie laughed. "I'm serious," she said. "Our entire future may depend on it." She went on in a rush of breath, not allowing Caroline to speak.

"A spot has opened up at Ohio State Law School and Ted has been invited to fill it. There's only forty- eight hours for him to decide. Ohio State," Jamie said again, re-emphasizing the name.

"That's good news," Caroline said. "What does it have to do with me."

"Classes start in three days."

"So?"

"We have no place to live and no time to find a place." Long silence. "Can we come and live with you?"

"What do you mean WE?"

"I plan to come with him. Finish up my last year with him."

Caroline was pacing by this time. Her hair was falling into her eyes. She pushed it back with a fist. "This is your senior year. Transferring will surely lose you some credit hours and push graduation out at least a semester." Caroline paused. "What about your job? I thought you loved working at The Electric Quilt."

"Mom, you're always saying you don't see enough of me. If I lived with you, that problem would be solved. Think about it. You'd love having us there."

Caroline was speechless. They'd worked so long and so hard to get this far.

"Mom?" Jamie said.

"No," Caroline finally said. "You have to graduate. You need to finish your degree."

"I will. It will just be at Ohio State instead of at Bowling Green."

Silence.

"Mom?"

Tears of frustration and fear began to flow down Caroline's cheeks. "No. You have to finish school. It's too late to make this change."

"Mom?" It was a plea.

"Have you talked to your father about this?"

"Not yet?" Jamie said, "But I know he won't say no."

"How do you know?"

Silence on the other end of the line.

"You know your dad has gone off the cliff in another direction."

"I know," Jamie almost whispered into the phone.

"None of us can depend on him right at the moment."

"Daddy loves us," Jamie said. "He wants us all to be happy."

"He's showing it in a really funny way at the moment, out there driving around in his new yellow Porsche convertible.

He's hanging out in bars , and only seeing Budd after school when I'm not around."

"Oh, Mom, I know it has to be awful. . . but,"

"But, nothing," Caroline said. "You have to finish your degree."

"I didn't want to tell you this over the phone, Mom. I wish you wouldn't make me."

"The only thing I want to make you do, is stay in school. Ted can stay with us till he finds another place, but you need to stay in school right where you are."

Jamie sucked in long breaths on the other end of the line. There was a hint of sniveling and not much else until she said, "You need to sit down, Mom."

"I do not need to sit down," Caroline said. "I need you to stop talking foolishness."

"Mom, Ted and I are going to have a baby." It came out in a rush of breath and tears.

Caroline couldn't respond. She dropped the phone and began to search the shop for a way out.

She rushed into the shop office, slammed the door behind her and dug through her purse till she found her cell phone. She hit an automatic dial button and clutched the phone to her ear. She wiped her tears as the phone rang for Charles, wherever he was.

He didn't answer. Caroline left a tearful message. "Call me as soon as you get this Charles. Call me. I need to talk to you about Jamie." She sucked in breath. "Call me or you'll be sorry."

Chapter 6

"What is it?" Nan said. Caroline had returned to the shop. Tears were still flowing down her cheeks. "Bad news?"

"The worst," Caroline sobbed.

Aggie moved in and put her arms around Caroline. "Is Jamie ill?" she asked.

"Oh Aggie," Caroline sobbed into her shoulder. She gasped before she spoke. "A baby. Jamie is having a baby."

"A baby? That's wonderful news. A precious little baby. Angie stepped back and clapped her work-worn hands together. "There's nothing like a baby to bring joy."

Nan held her hands together in a prayerful pose and rested them against her lips. "A baby," she crooned.

"She's not married," Caroline sobbed. "The baby has no daddy."

"Every baby has a daddy," Aggie said.

"I have to talk to Charles."

Nan nodded. "Did you call him," she asked.

"No answer," Caroline said. "Just like the last three times I called him."

"He'll call," Aggie said. "Charles is a good man."

Caroline gave her a shattering look. "Not so much lately."

Nan rubbed Caroline's shoulder. Aggie smiled as Caroline's phone began to play Dolly Parton singing Nine-to-Five."

It's Charles.

"Is Jamie okay?" he yelled. Caroline, Aggie and Nan could all hear him. Caroline moved the phone away from her ear.

"We have to talk, Charles. Can you meet me?" She turned to Nan. "What time is it?"

"4:20," Nan said.

"Meet me at Emilio's, will you?"

"Is Jamie okay?" Charles shouted again.

"No, she's not okay," Caroline sobbed into the phone. "That boy . . . the law student . . . Ted . . ."

"What about him? He's a Browns fan. How bad can he be? Has he done something to Jamie?"

"Oh Charles, she's going to have a baby."

There was silence on the other end of the line.

"Go home, Caroline. I'll meet you there in thirty minutes." Charles hung up.

"I knew he'd call," Aggie said. She patted Caroline who was shrugging into her jacket. "A grandmother, you're going to be a grandmother. This is wonderful news."

"Times have changed," Nan said. "Lots of women have babies without being married. It's almost more common than having a baby and being married."

"You're going to love being a grandmother." Aggie said. "It's better than peanut butter."

Caroline grabbed her purse and headed for the door. "Can you open in the morning, Nan? And load up the stuff to take to the encampment? I'll meet you there."

"Who will look after the shop?" Nan asked.

Caroline looked confused.

"The shop," Nan said. "If I meet you at the encampment, who will look after the shop?"

"I'll come in after opening, like I did this morning," Aggie said. "I can look after things till one of you gets back from the encampment."

"We could just skip it," Nan said.

"No, they're counting on us," Caroline said. "We have to go." She dug out her keys and headed out the door.

"I'd sure like to be a fly on the wall for this conversation," Aggie said.

Nan nodded and smiled. "Me, too."

Chapter 7

Charles was waiting in the living room when Caroline arrived. He had prepared her a stiff drink. He handed it to her after she tugged off her jacket and tossed it onto the couch. Tears were running down her cheeks.

"Oh Charles," she said. "They want to come here and live. Jamie wants to drop out of school. She says she will finish up at Ohio State." Caroline sucked in air. ". . . after the baby is born." She broke into a new set of gasping sobs. Charles shifted from foot to foot, clearly distraught himself. He looked tired and disheveled but Caroline didn't notice. She sipped her drink and coughed. "What is this?" she asked.

"Maker's Mark," Charles said. "I had it in my car."

"You're carrying booze in your car these days?"

"I'm living in my car these days," Charles said. He stepped forward and put his arms around Caroline. She sunk into their familiar comfort. When she realized what she was doing, she pulled away, took another sip of the Maker's Mark, then emptied the glass and handed it to Charles.

"What are we going to do?" Caroline watched while Charles refilled her glass and handed it back.

"I think the damage has already been done," he said. "Grandpa; grand dad, Pap paw. I kind of like the sound of it."

"How can you say that?" Caroline took another healthy pull on her refilled drink.

"Are you going to let the kids move in with you?"

"I told Jamie Ted can stay here till he finds another place. That was before she told me they were expecting a baby. A baby, Charles. Jamie is having a baby." She wiped her eyes and fell into Charles' arms again. "What are we going to do?"

"We're going to drive up to Bowling Green and talk to Jamie and Ted. We're going to ask them what their plans are.

They're going to be the parents of our grandchild. I think we should treat them like grown-ups."

"Jamie seems like a baby herself. Bringing her laundry home and always needing money for something or other. Does that sound like a grown-up?"

Charles stroked Caroline's hair and pushed it back off her face. "No, but becoming a mother trumps it all. We have to go talk with them."

"Right now?"

"We could wait until tomorrow," Charles said, "but soon. We need to go soon."

"I can't go tomorrow. I've made arrangements to sell kid's kits at the civil war encampment outside of town. Can you go, Charles? Would you do this for me?"

"It's for me, too, Caroline. Jamie is my daughter, too. Or have you forgotten?"

Caroline pulled away from him. Turned her back.

"I'll do it," he said. "But this is part of the problem between us. I feel like an outsider till you need something from me. I don't think you love me any more Caroline."

Caroline hurried past Charles' words like they hadn't been spoken. "You've got to talk her out of dropping out of school. She's so close to graduation."

"I can't promise anything. Jamie is almost as stubborn as you are." Charles smiled, but Caroline didn't.

We have to cooperate about this, no matter what problems there are between us. We just have to."

"Of course we have to cooperate. I'd do anything for you. I'd do anything for Jamie. We're related." Charles' forehead wrinkled. "Do you think I don't care about you anymore?"

"Why would I think that, Charles. You're living in your car. You're not the man I knew when we got married. I don't know what is wrong with you. I don't know what is wrong with Jamie," Caroline hesitated, took a breath, "except that she's pregnant and might be dropping out of school. I don't know anything, Charles."

Charles slipped an arm around Caroline's shoulders. "I'm kind of confused myself," he said. "I could stay the night if you want."

Caroline shrugged off Charles' arm. She put her hands on her hips, bit her lower lip. "Not a chance Charles. But, you will go talk to Jamie and Ted tomorrow?"

Charles studied his hands. "Yes," he answered. "I'll talk to them."

"Call me when you've spoken to them?"

"Yes."

Charles' shoulders slumped. He picked up the bottle of Maker's Mark from the coffee table, started toward the kitchen and the garage. He remembered his car wasn't in the garage, turned and left through the front door.

Caroline locked the door behind him and went upstairs to bed after she drained her glass.

Chapter 8

"I just love the pot holders," Melissa said. "I'm going to buy three sets of them. One for each of my granddaughters."

"Do your granddaughters cook?" Nan asked.

"No, but these are so cute and such good quilting practice." Melissa's grey roots were showing this morning. She badly needed a color touch up.

Caroline waved across the center of the encampment to Nan who already had the sale table set up outside the quilter's tent. Melissa was helping her spread kits out on the table. Clarissa stood between Nan and Melissa handing each one kits. The twins were dressed just alike again today. Homespun dresses that buttoned to the collar and were covered by white bibbed aprons. Melissa still looked fifteen years younger than Clarissa. Caroline decided it had to be Melissa's dyed hair.

Caroline carried a bag of quilting magazines and a red-work embroidery project. She planned to make good use of the time at the sale table today. Having her hands busy would help keep her from going crazy until she heard from Charles.

The re-enactors were going about their business in the camp – making up their beds and tents. Some were cooking breakfast over open fires and some were just kicked back and relaxing at their camp site. The mood was cozy and calm.

Kenny was pulling tables out and setting them up in front of his tent as Caroline walked past. He smiled and made a sweeping bow toward her. At just that moment Annie came out of the tent. She was yelling at Kenny and he was doing his best to ignore her. She was wearing her yellow Annie Oakley outfit.

"Where were you?" she yelled.

Kenny didn't answer. He continued to drag tables out of his tent and Caroline hurried on toward the quilter's tent. Annie yelled again, "Where were you?"

Caroline continued to walk but looked back over her shoulder to see what might happen next. She stumbled and dropped her red-work to the ground. Kenny hurried over to help her retrieve it and they nearly bumped heads as both bent over to pick up the embroidery.

Annie didn't come to help. She stepped back into the tent and watched from there. Her arms were crossed tightly across her chest.

Kenny handed the needlework to Caroline. "Remember you promised to come look at my goods today."

Caroline smiled and nodded. She glanced at Annie in the tent and smiled at her, too. Annie did not smile back. When Caroline got to the quilter's tent Melissa and Nan were watching the argument that was continuing in Kenny's tent. "What's that all about?"Caroline asked Melissa.

"Mmm, sort of a lover's quarrel," Melissa said.

"So they are an item?" Nan asked.

"At least Annie thinks so. Kenny is one of the nicest men in the world. He spreads himself thin among the divorcees and the widows in various encampments. He considers it a public service. But I think Clarissa is his favorite and Clarissa certainly thinks she is his favorite."

Caroline laughed. "With Charles gone, I have a new appreciation for that kind of public service. So why the argument?"

"Annie would like to monopolize the man's time. Her husband died three years ago from rabbit fever. It was all very sad. At first she talked about it like he was the only man who ever died."

"She must have loved him a lot," Nan said. She straightened a stack of kits that kept sliding to the side.

"Not so sure about that but his death was a shock," Melissa said. "It was a crazy random thing. Her husband trapped rabbits to keep them out of his garden in the spring. Used Have-A-Hart-Traps and carried the bunnies off to the country to release them. All very humane. Then as he was releasing one terrified little bunny, the bunny bit him. He didn't think much of it, put ointment on it and went on with his life. About two weeks later he got what he and Annie both thought was the flu. Fever, body aches, diarrhea – all the things that go with the flu. He didn't get better and by the time Annie got scared enough to take him to the doctor it was too late. He died."

"That's awful," Nan said.

"It was. The doctors said it was rabbit fever. I thought poor Annie would never stop grieving and feeling guilty." Melissa shook her head sadly. "So, when Clarissa's husband died, I started attending encampments with her to promote the relationship with Kenny and to protect her from unreasonable attachments. Single, older women are very vulnerable to that sort of thing. I didn't really help Clarissa much. She fell for Kenny hard. You may have noticed the tension created between her and Annie. "

"How has it worked out?" Caroline asked. "Doesn't your husband mind?"

"My husband golfs. I don't think he misses me at all. Kenny took Clarissa to supper a time or two, held her hand once in a while, and made her feel better about her widow-hood," Melissa said. "Clarissa is shy you know." Melissa cast a glance at her sister to see if she was listening. Her eyes never left the sale table.

"You weren't worried about Kenny?"

"No, Kenny wouldn't hurt a fly. He's a real gentleman."

Just at that moment a scream came from Kenny's tent and all three women looked in that direction. Kenny had his arms around Annie's waist and was carrying her out of the tent. She was kicking and trying to break loose. She did wiggle loose and fell to the dusty ground. She jumped up and it was obvious even from the distance that she had gotten her yellow cow girl suit all dirty. She brushed herself off and stomped away toward the blacksmith's shop where her display was located. Kenny looked at the three women by the quilting tent and shrugged his shoulders helplessly. He gave them an embarrassed grin and went back inside his tent.

"I think I'd tread softer with a women who is a sharp shooter," Caroline said to the two other women.

The first bus of the morning pulled into the parking area and released fifty running, curious fifth graders. It was going to be a long day.

Chapter 9

It was just past noon when Charles called from Bowling Green. "How is your sale going?"

"Never mind that, Charles, how is Jamie?"

"She and Ted are sitting right here with me. We're having a little lunch. I do have to say, Jamie looks radiant. She reminds me of you when you were pregnant with her."

"Oh Charles, how can you say that?"

"It's true, Caroline. It's really true. This is not the end of the world."

"If only they were married. That baby needs the love and protection of two parents, not just one."

"I know. I know. They plan to get married as soon as they get a moment."

"How could anything be more important right now?"

"Ted has to get to Columbus and get registered for his classes. Jamie does, too. She isn't planning to drop out of school, Caroline. She's just transferring for her senior year."

"When is all this supposed to happen? It's already September."

"They have only a few days to get everything done. That's why they have no time for a wedding."

"So?"

"So what?" Charles said.

"So what do the grown-ups have planned?"

"We're loading up the cars with everything they can carry and heading back to Buckeye Grove. We'll be there this evening."

"All of you?"

"Yes, all of us. Ted is going to stay at our house and get all of his matriculating done while he is there."

"How did I get to be the lucky one?"

"I can hardly have him move into my car with me, Caroline."

"Too bad you bought such a small sporty model. Otherwise it might work." Caroline said. "And what about Jamie? What's she going to do?"

"She's going to come back with us tonight. We'll unload and she'll go back to Bowling Green for another load of stuff tomorrow."

"What are we going to do with all this stuff, Charles? We don't have any place to store it."

"They're both leaving all the furniture with their roommates and just the soft goods are coming home. Bedding, a couple of lamps. Not as much as you are imagining."

"Still, what are we going to do with it?"

"It should fit in the garage."

Silence from Caroline.

"Are you there? Did we get cut off?"

"I'm here. I only wish I wasn't."

"It's a difficult situation, Caroline. It's better if we talk in person. Jamie is fine. Ted is fine. The baby is fine. She's due in December."

"It's a girl?"

"It's a girl," Charles said. "Jamie has been seeing a doctor and the baby is fit as a fiddle.

Caroline didn't speak, letting this news sink in. Knowing the baby – her granddaughter - was a girl made the news more real. It cracked her heart open and she could feel the love breaking loose.

She was quiet so long, Charles spoke again. "Caroline? It's going to be fine. We'll talk when we all get home. It's going to be a bit confusing and uncomfortable for a while, but we can do it. We really have no choice. Just wait till you see Jamie. She is absolutely glowing."

"Try not to overdo it, please. What time do you think you'll get back here?"

"We still have to load up the cars and pack the rest of the stuff Jamie is coming back for tomorrow. I guess we'll be there about five or six if we don't run into too much traffic."

"Okay Charles. I'll be here at the encampment till two or three and then back to the shop. I'll try to be home by the time you get there."

"Could you plan a little supper, Caroline. I know we'll all be famished by then."

Caroline sighed. "I guess so Charles. Maybe just some bacon and eggs."

"I love it when you cook breakfast for supper."

" Drive carefully," Caroline said but Charles was gone. The phone was buzzing in her ear.

Nan had just bagged up two potholders and handed them to a little red haired girl about nine. "So?" she asked Caroline.

"So. . . Charles is bringing Ted and Jamie home with two cars piled full of their stuff. They are storing it in my garage and could I please plan a little supper." Caroline's shoulders sagged and her head drooped.

"Oh, honey," Nan said and gathered Caroline into a tight hug. "It will be fine. You'll see.

You're going to love having Jamie home. I know how much you miss her. And think of it. A sweet little baby."

"A baby girl," Caroline said. "It's a little girl."

Nan clapped her hands. "That's wonderful. It's going to be more than fine. You'll see."

"You're forgetting Ted," Caroline said.

"You know you like Ted. You told me so yourself last time he was in town."

"That was before." She sounded like she might cry again.

Chapter 10

Caroline and Nan packed up to go back to the shop a little after two. The last school bus had been loaded up with children and the encampment quieted down considerably. Melissa stopped by their table. "How did your day go?" she asked.

"We sold twenty-two pot holders and three aprons," Nan said.

"That many?" Melissa asked. "A pretty good day then."

"A very good day," Caroline said. "I wonder where kids get all the money they have to spend."

"From their parents, of course," Nan said. Melissa laughed.

"I'm sure you're right," Caroline said. Then to Melissa, "We have to get back to the shop and work on more kits for tomorrow. Thank you so much for inviting us to come out here."

"You're welcome," Melissa said. "We are finishing up the next to the last quilt of the season inside the tent. Tomorrow you'll have to add a few stitches."

"What do you do with the finished quilts?" Nan asked.

"We give them to civic groups for raffles and other fund raising events."

"What a wonderful way to spread the word about your group and quilting."

"We think so," Melissa said.

"Besides that we've scheduled Shelah to speak to our guild about civil war quilts. I'm looking forward to it. I may even expand the reproduction fabric section at the shop."

"Good idea," Melissa said. "This is part of the benefit of having this quilting display at the encampment. It generates interest in the art of quilting."

Caroline changed the subject. "I'm curious. Kenny never opened his tent his afternoon. Is it normal for people to come and go as they please?"

"Well, yes," Melissa said. "Everyone is a volunteer so it's sort of hard to insist on a schedule. But it is also unusual for him to be closed while the children are here. I wonder if the yelling match he had with Annie had anything to do with it."

"I wondered, too," Caroline said. "I missed having him here."

I suppose Annie was over to visit," Melissa said. "She seems to be everywhere."

"She was," Nan said. "What a talker that woman is."

"Yes," Caroline said. "I wondered about the attendance code," Caroline said. "I'm having a small family emergency and might not be able to get here every single day. Nobody would care about that?"

"We'd all care," Melissa said. She wrapped an arm around Caroline and gave her a hug. "But nobody will be keeping track of your every appearance. You might want to plan to come on Saturday morning or Sunday afternoon. Those times are especially busy."

"Thanks for the tip," Caroline said. Then she and Nan picked up their tote bags and Caroline wheeled the suitcase toward the Buick. Annie was standing in front of the blacksmith shop talking to a couple of ladies dressed in home spun dresses. Nan waved to her and she waved back. Kenny's tent was still tightly closed.

Aggie and Goldie were working on potholder kits back at the shop while they visited. Aggie cut the pieces and Goldie stuffed them into their individual bags. There were no customers.

"It's a good thing we went to the encampment today," Caroline said.

"Only three customers all day long," Aggie said.

"And I'm between manicures, so I decided to come over and keep Aggie company," Goldie said. "Robert is taking me out for supper at the new Coney dog restaurant this evening."

"I didn't know we had a new Coney dog restaurant."

"The other side of town," Goldie said. "Robert loves Coney dogs."

"Sounds like fun," Nan said. She sighed. "I'll be so happy when Stan gets home and the two – she corrected herself – three of us can go for a Coney dog."

"Maybe I should pick some up for supper," Caroline said.

Aggie looked at her quizzically. "Charles, Jamie and Ted are going to be here for supper," Caroline said.

"He's bringing them home?" Aggie asked.

"Yes. We're going to talk. . ." Tears formed in the corners of Caroline's eyes.

"The baby is a girl," Nan said.

"Awww, a little girl," Aggie said. Tears rolled down Caroline's cheeks. Aggie pulled her into her arms and patted her shoulder.

Caroline and Nan returned to the work of cutting patterns and stuffing them into small plastic bags

"When will Stan be home?" Aggie said to Nan.

"Six more days," Nan said with a smile.

"I like the idea of having that boy around again," Aggie said. "He's been in the middle east long enough." Nan and Stan had started a romance before he left to fulfill his military obligation. You might even say they had fallen in love. Stan worked for UPS when he wasn't fighting a war some place. He stopped at the shop nearly every day making a delivery of some kind.

"I can't argue with that," Nan said. "I can hardly wait. He's in Texas right now and my stress level is down about a mile since he got back on America soil. He can call me every day now."

"That's nice." Caroline said. "But I'd hate to pay the bill."

"It's not as bad as you think. I've finished up Jack's quilt and it's ready to give to him when his dad gets home."

"He's going to love it," Aggie said. "With all those dogs on it."

Nan smiled. "Stan told me he might buy Jack a dog when he gets home."

"A six-year-old needs a dog," Aggie said.

"How's his mother going to feel about that?" Caroline asked. She handed Nan a set of table runner pieces and lay down her rotary cutter. It was a cutter that was designed to cut through heavy fabrics, like fleece and chenille. Caroline liked it for big projects because it would cut through several layers at a time.

Nan stuffed the pieces into a bag and stapled it shut. "Stan is going to keep the dog at his house. It won't be a bit of trouble for Jack's mother."

"What kind of a dog is Stan getting?" Caroline asked.

"Not sure," Nan said. "Maybe a shepherd of some sort."

"If I was getting a dog for a little boy, I'd get a collie that looked just like Lassie," Aggie said. "I liked that program on television."

"Charles always wanted a collie," Caroline said and mentally added it to the list of unfulfilled desires in Charles's life.

Chapter 11

Caroline stopped at the grocery store on the way home to pick up bacon, eggs, a loaf of bread and two bottles of wine. It could be a long night. When she arrived home she found a note from her younger daughter on the kitchen counter:

Dear Mom,

Nick and I have gone to a movie.

Don't wait up.

Love, Budd

Budd's cryptic notes were almost all the communication Caroline had with her younger daughter since Charles moved out. Caroline thought she might be mad. She also thought she might be on Charles' side. With Budd at the movie, Caroline wouldn't have to tolerate her eyeballs rolling at everything she and Charles said to one another and she wouldn't be faced with the prospect of asking Nick to leave while the family discussion took place. Nick was the son of her landlord Schultz, a student at Ohio State University and much too worldly for Budd who was a high school senior this year. Not that anybody cared what Caroline thought.

The kitchen was still a mess. Caroline stowed her purchases in the fridge and stuffed dirty dishes into the dish washer. She took a swipe at the counter with a dish cloth. Who knew how long it had been in use. She thought she'd made some improvement by the time she heard laughter from the garage. Was she the only one who just wanted to cry and cry?

Charles came into the kitchen first. "We're here," he said to Caroline. Jamie was second in line. She hurried to her mother and threw her arms around her. Caroline had no choice but to hug her back. Ted came in last and he wisely made no move to be affectionate.

"We've had the best day, Mom," Jamie said. "I'm so glad you had Dad come up. He was such a big help, though I'd rather he still had the SUV, instead of that cute little roller skate."

Charles and Ted laughed. Caroline did not. "I think I'll be able to get the rest of our things in Ted's car tomorrow."

Caroline began cooking bacon and taking egg orders. "Can you get the toast, Jamie?" she asked and Jamie hurried to help. Charles and Ted made themselves comfortable at the table talking about football and how Ohio State might do this year; whether or not Ted might be able to get tickets.

Caroline kept her cool at the stove, only once having to resist bashing Charles in the head with the hot bacon skillet.

Ted asked for two more eggs and Jamie popped up from her seat to make him more toast. Even Caroline could see there were some wonderful things about being young and in love. Charles had learned to make his own toast.

Nobody mentioned the baby, so Caroline finally had to do it. "You know a baby deserves to have both a mother and a father on its side. From the very beginning. Putting off the wedding is not good for any of you"

Ted swabbed his plate with the last of his toast and put it in his mouth. "We plan to get married, Mrs. Clarkson," he said. "There are some other things that have to come first with my change to Ohio State for law school."

"Things are already dismally out of order as far as I can see," Caroline said. "And what about Jamie's school? Hers is as important as yours. Maybe more so since she is going to have a baby to look after."

"Mother, this isn't all Ted's fault and I sure don't expect you to take it out on him. "

"Take it out on him? I'm not taking it out on anyone." Caroline defended herself. It was clear nobody else was going to do it.

"You have no idea how important and exciting it is that Ted has the opportunity to graduate from Ohio State Law School. Yes, there are a few hoops to jump through but in the end it will all be worth it. You'll see." Jamie yawned and stretched her hands over her head before Caroline could respond. "I'm exhausted," she said. "I have to be up and headed north early tomorrow."

"I don't think you should be lifting and carrying heavy stuff in your condition," Caroline said to Jamie.

"I'll be fine, Mom. But I do think Ted and I should get some rest."

"You can use Budd's room," Caroline said. "She'll be late and Ted can sleep alone in your room."

Jamie rolled her eyes. "Moth—er" she said with the pained voice children often reserve for their parents. "We sleep together all the time."

"Too much information," Caroline said. "This is still my house and I don't care how often you sleep together in Bowling Green. Here, we go by my rules. There is no sleeping together till there is a wedding."

Charles cleared his throat. "It's my house, too and I think you're being silly. Besides the damage is done."

"I don't care what you think, Charles. They want to live here? They will do it my way."

"What about Budd? She'll have a heart attack if she starts to crawl into bed and finds me there," Jamie said.

"I'll leave her a note," Caroline said. Jamie turned on her toe and headed out of the room.

Ted stood up. "Sorry for all the trouble, Mrs. Clarkson. We really do appreciate your allowing us to stay here. Jamie will be better in the morning." He stuttered to get the next part out. "She's been pretty high strung . . . since we found out about the . . . baby."

Caroline gave him a glare that would ignite coal. He turned and hurried out of the kitchen.

"You've got to give them a break. They have lots of things to take care of in a very short time."

"Charles, I don't have to do anything. I'm letting them stay here for right now. I think that's enough." Charles shrugged. "I have a big day tomorrow, too. We're selling kits at the civil war encampment again."

"Okay, I can take a hint." Charles stood. "How did it go today?"

"Pretty well actually. We sold all but two of the kits we had and had to go back to the shop and make up more for tomorrow."

"Good," Charlie said. "Very good." He leaned toward Caroline to give her a kiss and she turned her head. "Oh, sorry," Charles said and went out through the garage door. Caroline could hear the door go down as she locked the kitchen door behind Charles. She hoped Budd had taken her key.

Caroline finished wiping off the counters and then she started the dishwasher. Supper dishes had filled it up. She sat down at the table again, wrote the note to Budd warning her that her sister was in her bed. Then she lay her head on her crossed arms and sobbed . . . well, like a baby.

Chapter 12

Nan was all packed and ready to go to the encampment when Caroline arrived at Always in Stitches. Kathy was there to cover the shop while they were gone. They had forty kits to sell and were looking forward to a profitable day. Caroline was only mildly exhausted from the emotional encounter last night with people she loved. Not including Ted.

They drove Nan's car to the encampment as Ted was borrowing Caroline's to drive to OSU to take care of enrollment business. They had the rolling suitcase and a large box of kits. "Wait here," Nan said as she pulled the rolling suitcase from the trunk. I'll be right back to help you with the box."

"I think I can get it," Caroline said. She pulled the box from the back seat and hefted it to test the weight. "No problem. I can get this," she said but Nan was already halfway to the quilting tent and didn't hear a word. Caroline hoisted the box and managed to get her arm around it and lift it. She managed to carry the box part of the way when it began to slip from her arms. She tightened her grip and hurried a bit. She was right in front of the sales tent when the bottom fell open on the box and potholder kits fell out the bottom of the box, all over the dirty, dusty ground. "Damn!" she said louder than she should have.

"Looks like you've got a problem there," Kenny said as he hurried to help her. He was wearing a blue plaid shirt today and it brought the blue out of his grey eyes. Caroline could tell this even from her squatting position picking up kits. She smiled up at him.

"Good to see you. I missed you yesterday."

"I take a mental health day now and again," Kenny said. "Stress, you know."

"Yes, I do know," Caroline said. "Glad you could get away for a break."

"Looks like you can use a break right this minute." Caroline laughed and Kenny reached out a hand to help her stand.

"The bottom fell out of the blasted box," Caroline said. " Thank goodness the kits are in plastic bags or they would be as dirty as the ground. She brushed off one of the bags. "We can clean them off, except for maybe a few." Caroline began picking up the kits and brushing them off one by one. She had an armload of them before Kenny brought forth a cart with wheels and took the kits from her arms and laid them on the cart. "Thank you, oh thank you so much," Caroline said.

"Anything to help a lady in distress," Kenny said. He lowered his hat in a sweeping bow. Caroline was forced to giggle by his uncommon gesture. He took her hand and kissed it lightly.

Nan got back to them at just that moment. She looked from one of them to the other.

"The bottom fell out of your box?" Nan asked.

"It sure did," Kenny said. He grinned broadly. "But we've got it taken care of now. Let me push the cart over to your tent." He began to do just that. The tires screeched and the cart jiggled the quilting kits as it rolled across the dry, dusty ground.

"Thanks," Caroline said. "You're a lifesaver."

"That's just what I am. And I'll save yours every chance I get." His eyes twinkled and Caroline turned to begin moving the kits to the table Nan had pulled outside the quilting tent. "No hurry with the cart," he said. "Whenever you're finished just bring it back over." He walked back toward his tent.

"I think he's sweet on you," Nan said.

"He can't be sweet on me. I'm married," Caroline said but she smiled when she said it.

It was another good day for Caroline and Nan at their make-shift shop. Annie came to visit about one o'clock. It was after her first demonstration of the day. Caroline had heard the sound of gunshots just before Annie showed up. Her presence caused the little girls to crowd around her and Caroline's quilting booth. Annie was wearing her pink cowgirl suit today. By the time the children began to get back on their busses only two apron kits and six potholder kits were left. They were going to have to work extra tonight to make kits for tomorrow. It made no sense to miss out on the good sales they were having. Caroline was thinking she might have to ask her sister and her mom to help with cutting kits over the week end. They didn't mind helping out when she was in a bind. She needed to get a little lead on the sales. It was such a nice problem to have.

Kenny hurried toward Caroline as she was leaving the encampment. He took her arm and pulled her to a stop. "You haven't looked at my wares, yet." he said. "You told me you would stop by and that was three days ago.

"I'm having a little family emergency", she told him. "I have to get home. Can you give me another chance later?"

"I guess so," Kenny said. "But you have to promise to let me buy you lunch tomorrow."

Caroline sighed. "I have to tell you, Kenny, I'm married. At least I think I still am married."

Kenny threw back his head and laughed a hearty laugh. "I have no lecherous tendencies," he said. "I swear. I'd just like to know you better."

"Okay. We'll have lunch tomorrow. I promise, but right now I have to get home." She turned away from him to emphasize the point.

He patted her shoulder. "It's a date," he said.

Caroline lay her head back on the driver's seat of Nan's car. It had been a long, busy day. The very best part of all was she hadn't thought about Jamie, her baby and that Ted boy once today. She had been too busy. It was a relief.

Kathy and Aggie had been working on kits all day long. They had two boxes full of aprons and pot holders. Caroline dug out a second suitcase on wheels and filled it with kits. It was older and a bit ratty on the corners but much better than the boxes that had lost their bottoms earlier in the day.

Nan was expecting a call from Stan in Texas and she decided to hurry on home to take the call there. Caroline stayed at the shop and cut kits for an hour before she decided to head home and see what was happening there. She had to call Ted to come and pick her up since he had her car. She wasn't happy about having to depend on him.

Ted arrived in twenty-five minutes. "Sorry it took me so long Mrs. Clarkson. I got lost on the way."

"How could you get lost?" Caroline walked to the driver's side door and waited for Ted to get the idea she intended to drive. He climbed out of the car and walked to the passenger side and got back in.

"If you remember, I've only been to your shop twice before and I had Jamie to point the way both times."

"Oh," Caroline said. She wasn't giving the young man an inch.

Chapter 13

Budd and Nick were in the kitchen when Caroline arrived home. They had a bag of tortilla chips and a bowl of salsa on the table in front of them. Nick was eating them like it was his first meal. Charles arrived shortly after Caroline and Ted. "Has anyone heard from Jamie?" he asked after he poured himself a cup of coffee.

"She's on the road," Ted said. "I heard from her when she got to this side of Findlay. She should be here soon."

"Could someone please tell me what's going on here?" Budd said. "I nearly died when I climbed into my bed last night and Jamie was there."

"Didn't you see my note?" Caroline asked.

"What note?"

"This one," Caroline said. She picked up last night's note from the kitchen counter. It was still right where she had left it.

"I'm transferring to Ohio State for law school," Ted said.

Budd tilted her head to one side. She had a quizzical look on her face. "And?"

Ted responded. "I'm staying with your mom and dad till I find a place of my own." Charles sipped his coffee and nodded.

"And? That has what to do with my sister?"

Caroline was rattling pans, taking steps toward cooking up some burgers for supper.

"She's moving with me." Ted said.

Budd looked from Ted to her mother who had her head sticking into the refrigerator with her behind sticking into the air. "And?" Budd said.

Caroline slammed the refrigerator door and stood with her hands on her hips almost, but not quite, glaring at Ted. His face flushed red but he didn't speak. Just in the nick of time they heard the garage door going up. "That must be Jamie," Charles said.

Ted hurried to the door between the kitchen and the garage and opened it. Jamie walked into his arms and they kissed. Caroline turned her back. "Okay," Budd said. "What is going on around here?"

Silence filled the room. Nobody moved except Nick who continued to munch chips and salsa.

"Nick needs to leave?" Caroline said. "This is family business and I don't think we should discuss this in front of him."

"I don't think that's necessary," Charles said.

"Well, I do and I happen to be in charge of the house while you're off having a mid-life crisis on the streets."

Charles lowered his eyes and sipped his coffee. Budd elbowed Nick. He picked up the tortilla bowl and salsa and headed for the living room.

"Well?" Budd asked.

"Your sister and Ted are expecting a baby," Charles said. The parents-to-be smiled at one another. Caroline turned and stuck her head back in the refrigerator.

"A baby?" Budd clapped her hands and yelled. "Wow! A baby!" She hurried to her sister and gave her a hug. She patted Ted on the shoulder. "Way to go, Ted."

"It's a girl," Jamie said. Then she clapped her hands and jumped up and down with Budd.

"I'm going to be an aunt." Budd grinned. "I may learn to knit." She scanned the room. "So, is Dad coming home? We'll be one big, happy family again."

Caroline turned. Her arms were full of condiments. "Not on your life," she said.

Chapter 14

Charles drove Caroline to work next morning. He had spent the night on the couch and Ted needed Caroline's car again. His was still full of all Jamie's worldly goods. She planned to spend the day unpacking.

Nan hadn't arrived yet so Caroline opened things up and turned on the cash register and filled it with the day's change. She returned three bolts of fabric to their shelves and sighed. Her life was careening out of control.

Nan burst through the shop's back door. "Stan was given an early release," she said. He'll be home tomorrow." She was smiling broadly.

Caroline wasn't sure how many more ecstatic young women she could stand. "That's wonderful," she said. "I guess you'll want the day off."

"No he won't be home till late afternoon – about 5 o'clock. He plans to see Jack first thing and spend some time with him. Maybe take him to supper. Then he'll come to my apartment and we'll get re-acquainted."

"Ah,"

"I'll probably be happier working than sitting at home chewing my nails while I wait. But I would like to have Saturday off. Can we work that out?"

"Of course," Caroline said. "I knew this was going to happen when Stan came home. I'll see if Kathy can come in? If she can't I'll ask Aggie. She's as good as an employee by this time. Best thing is she's free."

"Best thing is, she's Aggie," Nan said.

Caroline laughed. "You're right. I'm so happy to have her around. But still, the bottom line is looking pretty lean and I have to think about that."

Caroline loaded up the rolling suitcase with sewing kits. She added the change box and her red work project. "I need to borrow your car again today. Ted still is using mine."

"No problem." She was already cutting kits but stopped long enough to toss Caroline the keys.

"I'll put some gas in before I bring it back." Nan smiled and went back to her work.

Things were moving slowly at the encampment. The sky was grey with a cover of wet looking clouds. The rain was holding off, still Caroline thought she'd have to set up her table inside the quilting tent today. There were no busses in the parking area and no children running between buildings. Caroline liked the children

Caroline walked past Kenny's tent. He was watching her pull the rolling suitcase. "Can I help you with that?" he called.

"No thanks, I've got it."

"Don't forget we're having lunch today. I'll stop by and pick you up about 12:30," Kenny said. "Hope the rain holds off." He cast a wary look at the sky and went back inside his tent.

Melissa and Clarissa were having an animated discussion in the rear of the tent. Shelah was arranging chairs around the quilting frame. "I think I'll talk about popular civil war patterns when I visit your guild."

"That sounds interesting. Aggie told me at least one of our members is making a signature quilt which was popular back in the day."

"Yes, it was a way to send the family into war with the soldiers who left home to fight."

"Hmmm," Caroline said. "I'm eager to hear what you have to say. I think our members will learn a lot. Michael, one of our favorite guild members has unearthed a civil war era quilt he'd like to have assessed."

"How exciting," Shelah said. She went back to arranging chairs around the table. When she had them the way she wanted them she sat down and bent her head over the quilt and began to stitch.

"I'm setting up inside this morning. Is that okay?" Caroline said to nobody in particular.

"Good idea," Shelah said without looking up. "It sure looks like rain."

The children arrived and the pace picked up. A trio of third grade girls bought kits from Caroline. They hung around her table and circled the quilting frame four times before they left the tent. Four women arrived and began working on the quilt in progress. Melissa and Clarissa stopped arguing in the back of the tent. Melissa took a seat at the quilting frame and Clarissa hurried past Caroline on her way out of the tent. She had tears running down her cheeks.

The morning passed quickly and before Caroline knew it she began hearing the gunfire from Annie's demonstration. Soon Kenny was standing in front of her table. "Are you hungry yet?" he asked.

"Yes," she said. "I think I am."

Kenny smiled a white-toothed smile at her. "Good" he said.

Caroline threw a sheet over her table to indicate she was closed. Kenny extended an arm toward her. She hesitated only a moment before she took it and allowed him to lead her to the food tent.

It was good to have him beside her. She could feel the muscles in his forearm. She liked having a man pay attention to her. She missed Charles. She hated Charles. It was like being a teenager again.

The rain was still holding back but a fine damp mist hung in the air. The food tent was busy with children buying soda and candy. Kenny ordered soup beans and cornbread talking over the children's heads. It was the only choice.

"Authenticity," Kenny said. "Civil war soldiers were lucky if they had food this good to eat. "

Caroline smiled. They took a picnic table under a tent fly. Kenny took a seat across from her. "So," Kenny said, "tell me how it happens that you're not sure if you're married." He took off his hat and set it on the table.

Caroline hemmed and hawed and couldn't quite figure out how to explain her situation.

"Sounds like a mid-life crisis to me. Does he have another woman?"

Caroline eyes opened wider. "I never really thought of that?" she said. "Charlie would never cheat on me. I did see him with a young woman in his car one day, but . . . she was the age of our daughter."

"Sounds like he is confused, or weary or in the midst of a mid-life crisis," Kenny counted off the possibilities.

"I guess you're right."

"My wife died five years ago," he said. "Pancreatic cancer. She fought as long as she was able. It was a very hard death for both of us." Kenny slathered butter on a piece of corn bread and popped it in his mouth. "The older I get the more friends and relatives I lose. It's depressing."

"Charles isn't dead, he's just gone. Gone is better than dead." Caroline reached across the table and patted Kenny's arm. She wanted to help. She wanted him to feel better. "Tell me about her." Kenny gave her a quizzical look. "Your wife."

"She was a peach," he said. "I never loved anybody else. She made me promise to spread myself thin among the widows and divorcees when she was gone."

"I don't understand," Caroline said.

"She said older single women were the most overlooked segment of society. She wanted me to pay attention to them."

"Very generous of her." Caroline said.

"She didn't tell me how to keep them from fighting over me. It's quite a dilemma really. I never imagined it would be. I'm not exactly Prince Charming." He spread his arms out to show Caroline how far from Prince Charming he was.

"I like you," she said. "And I think it's honorable of you to try to fulfill your wife's dying wishes."

"Maybe," Kenny said. "Maybe. But it's led to some . . . what do the politicians call them . . . unintended consequences."

Caroline laughed and so did Kenny. Caroline decided she liked this man more than she probably should.

The clouds were breaking up by the time Caroline returned to her table by the quilting tent. Annie Oakley was waiting for her there. She was wearing her blue cowgirl suit.

"I came to invite you to watch my shooting demonstration today."

"I'd like that," Caroline said. "I forget what time you told me."

"5:00," Annie said. "Behind the blacksmith's shop."

Caroline looked at her watch. It was already two. She'd been at lunch longer than she thought. "Afraid I can't today. I have Nan's car and she's expecting her fellow home from a

middle east deployment. She hasn't seen him in six months."

"No, you don't want to make her late for that," Annie said. She shuffled her feet and brushed a bit of dust from her blue skirt. "I saw you having lunch with Kenny."

"Yes," Caroline said. "He seems like a very nice gentlemanly sort."

"That's what I used to think, but he's broken my heart."

"In what way?"

"I thought he cared about me. He took me to dinner. He took me to the movie. He even visited me in Huntington last winter. Then when Clarissa turned up single this spring, he started to wine and dine her."

"Were you going steady or engaged?" Caroline asked.

"I thought we were an item."

"What did Kenny think?"

"We never really talked about it, but the way he acted . . . I thought we were something special."

"Did he stop seeing you then?"

"Well, no. He still took me to supper a few times this summer, but I know he's seeing Clarissa now and again. There may even be another woman he sees."

"Another re-enactor?" Caroline asked.

"I'm not sure, but I'm pretty sure he is two-timing me and maybe three-timing me. I don't like it."

"He seems nice enough to me," Caroline said. "If you have no agreement, you probably don't have much to say about who he sees."

"Are you married?"

"Sort of."

"How can you be sort of married?"

"My husband and I are separated. But since my daughter came home from college he's sleeping on the couch at my house." Annie was listening intently. "It's complicated." Caroline said.

"Sounds like it." Annie said. "If it gets uncomplicated – like if you and your husband split – keep your hands off Kenny."

"Huh?"

"You heard me. In the meantime, I'd like you to come see my shooting demonstration. It will give you an idea of what you're up against. "

"Huh?" Caroline said again. She stood at the table watching Annie leave the tent and turn toward the blacksmith shop.

Chapter 15

"And then she threatened me." Caroline said.

She was relating her day to Jamie. They were sharing a hot chocolate in the kitchen. Jamie had her hair covered with a Bowling Green bandana. She had been unpacking the car and storing her belongings and Ted's in the garage.

"That's weird," Jamie said. She looked tired. "I'd never threaten another woman over Ted. I might threaten Ted, but not the woman."

Caroline laughed. "That's my girl." She sipped her cocoa. "Is everything unpacked and stowed?"

Jamie nodded.

"Good, I really need my car back. Stan may be home even as we speak. Nan is taking some time off to get reacquainted with him and I won't have her car to go to the encampment."

"Maybe I could come and help in the shop while Nan is off with Stan."

"That would be wonderful," Caroline said. "But first I need you to get your classes lined up. I will not sit quietly by while you lose out on your senior year of college. We've both worked too hard to get you where you are."

"I know, Mom. It's important to me, too. But I do have to think about Ted and the baby."

"Think about them all you want," Caroline said. "But it's more important than ever that you get your education. This baby is going to be depending on you and what if it turns out Ted can't be trusted to do the job? What if he takes off?"

"You mean like Dad?"

"Maybe. " Caroline looked up to the ceiling. It was covered in cobwebs. "You girls are nearly raised. Our parenthood job is nearly finished. Yours is just beginning, no matter what Ted decides along the way."

"So," Jamie said. "Are you interested in this Kenny guy?"

"Changing the subject? Okay. He's a very nice guy. Before she died, his wife made him promise to be nice to older, single women and make them feel important. He's tried to do this and now he's in the middle of jealous cat fights. It would be funny if it weren't so sad." Caroline sipped her cocoa and made a face. "Cold," she said and took it to the sink to dump it.

Ted came home at just that moment. "I'm registered," he said as he walked in from the garage. "I didn't know we had that much stuff," he said to Jamie. "I could barely get your mother's car into the garage."

Jamie hugged him enthusiastically and planted a kiss on his lips. Caroline looked away but not before she noticed the beginnings of a tiny baby bump on Jamie's stomach.

Stan's homecoming took everybody's breath away. Nan was out of the shop every possible moment. Caroline continued her days at the encampment and Aggie and Kathy covered the shop which was not pressuring anyone to work harder. Thank goodness there were children's kits to be made. It gave Aggie and Kathy something to do while they manned the shop.

Caroline was enjoying the children who visited the encampment. She helped a few of them start the kits they bought and when things got slow, she went to the quilting frame and added a few stitches. She and Kenny had lunch again but there were no more threatening visits from Annie. In fact there were no more visits at all.

Charles was still sleeping on the couch at 2908. Nobody knew how long he might stay. Jamie got registered at Ohio State. She signed up for fifteen hours which would delay her graduation only one semester. Caroline gratefully sent the tuition check and hoped for the best.

She wrote the check out of her shop account and it took her balance below $500. Not enough to pay next month's rent.

On Friday, Stan and Nan brought Jack into the shop. Caroline was preparing to leave for the encampment. Jack was six. He had blond fly-away hair that spiked and peaked when he got excited and sweaty. He was an active little boy and obviously very happy to have his dad home. He had a collie-colored ball of fur on the end of a leash. It was his new puppy turning herself inside out trying to get loose and sniff everybody's knees. Stan was hugged and kissed by Caroline and Aggie. Tears flowed at the homecoming.

"So glad you're home," Aggie said. "We missed you and Jack around here." She turned the six year old this way and that. "Look at how this boy has grown," she said. Jack smiled broadly and hugged his dad's waist while holding on to the puppy's leash.

"What's her name?" Caroline asked.

Jack looked at his dad, then back at Caroline. "Lassie," he said. His dad nodded and so did Jack.

"Lassie it is," Stan said. "We were having trouble deciding but when you start introductions, the name you use has stuck."

"I have to go," Caroline said. "I'm already late. The busses will be arriving before I get set up for the day."

"Let us drive you?" Nan asked. "I want Jack to see the encampment."

"What a good idea." Caroline looked at Stan who nodded his approval. "So, let's get going." They left the shop out the back door amid much hugging and many smiles and here and there a little puppy yelp. It was good to have Stan home.

Jacks face was pasted to the back side window as they drove into the encampment. Lassie was sitting in his lap licking the window. Caroline was right, she was late. There were already two busses in the parking lot and she could see children running in the village.

She hurried out of the car and Stan removed her rolling suitcase from the back of the car. "I'll get this," he said. "You go ahead."

Caroline went on to the quilting tent, waving to Kenny as she hurried past his tent. The crowd was mostly ten-year-olds this morning. They were swarming the bow and arrows and the pop guns. Kenny only looked away from the children for a second when Caroline hurried by. He waved and then turned his attention back to the boys.

Stan and Jack were swiveling heads looking this way and that. "This is really neat," Stan said. Jack's puppy was tugging at her leash and chasing after the little boys who were walking past. Stan bent and picked the dog up so the boys wouldn't tease her.

"Plan to stay at least till noon," Caroline said. "I'll close down the table and we'll all go watch Annie Oakley's shooting demonstration. I haven't seen it yet myself."

"We'd like that," Stan said. "We'll be back here to pick you up."

"I'll be ready," Caroline said and turned her attention to a blonde girl who was sorting through the kits. The girl had long pigtails that fell over her shoulders. Her lips were heart-shaped and glistening. She struck Caroline as a perfect little girl. Whatever that might be.

"Do I need a sewing machine to make the pot holders?" the little girl asked.

"No," Caroline said. "All the sewing can be done by hand."

"Would you help me?" The child smiled winningly at Caroline. She seemed used to having her wishes fulfilled.

"Yes, I can do that. You open the package and lay the pieces out on the table. I've got a spare needle and thread in my sewing kit. I'll find it and we'll get started."

Caroline liked the little girl. She was very polite and Caroline couldn't help but think that in a few years Jamie's baby, Caroline's grand baby, might be needing help with her sewing. She smiled at the picture she had in her head. She wasn't even born yet but Caroline wanted to pass along an important part of her life. If only her mother and father would find the time for a wedding.

The little blonde girl's name was Lily. Her mother was a teacher whose second grade class had been to the encampment the previous week. She told Lily she'd like a potholder for Christmas and had sent extra money so Lily could buy one. Lily and Caroline laid out the potholder pieces. Caroline showed Lily how to manage a thimble so she wouldn't poke holes in her fingers though it was too big and kept falling off. Caroline stuffed a scrap of fabric into the thimble to make it fit Lily's finger better. They began sewing pieces together. Caroline worked on one side and Lily on the other. The pieces went together quickly and easily. Then Caroline showed Lily how to fit the heat resistant batting into a small quilt sandwich with the stitched together pieces taking the part of the bread. She pinned the pieces together just as she noticed Nan, Stan, Jack and Lassie walking toward them.

"I threw a tomahawk," Jack said. He was jumping up and down with excitement. "It stuck in the log."

"Wow!" Caroline said, trying to share the boy's excitement. "Are you ready to watch the sharp-shooter show?"

"Yes, yes." Jack said.

Caroline turned back to Lily. "I have to close up my table," she said.

"Oh," Lily said. "I could watch things for you."

"Don't you want to look around with your friends?"

"No. I want to finish my mother's pot holder. Won't she be surprised when I bring it home this evening all finished?"

"She will," Caroline said. "Okay, you can watch my table, if you're sure."

"I'm sure," the child said.

Caroline left the child in charge and went toward the blacksmith shop with a lot of other folks who were headed that way for the show.

There were ropes to control the crowd and keep them out of the shooting area. Bright colored strips of plastic were tied to the ropes and flapped in the breeze.

Targets were positioned on a fence about forty feet from the shooting station which was just on the other side of the rope. The noise level was high and teachers did their best to control the children.

Caroline liked the rambunctiousness of the little boys. Some of them were drawing imaginary guns from imaginary holsters and pow-powing their friends. Jack watched all the activity but didn't take part. Stan was carrying the puppy to save her from being trampled by the crowd of children. It seemed a moderately dangerous place even before Annie took center stage for her firearm demonstration.

When she did come out she had on her pink fringed outfit. And Caroline had to give her credit. She was a showman. She twirled across the grass causing the fringe to dance about her body. She had guns in her hands and was shooting into the air. Pow! Pow! Pow!

Silence descended on the crowd and the children stood frozen with all eyes on Annie. Stan, Nan. Jack and Caroline had worked their way up to the front of the crowd so Jack could see the demonstration from a prime spot. Annie spoke to the children about the real Annie Oakley. She told them about Annie's travels with Buffalo Bill's Wild West Show; her marriage to a fellow sharp shooter, Frank Butler; and the fact she was born and died in Ohio. The children listened raptly.

And finally the shooting began. Annie cleared several targets off the fence in the distance. She shot a pretzel out of the mouth of the blacksmith. She had him throw a handful of playing cards into the air and she shot each one of them before it hit the ground.

"Wow," Stan said. "That woman is better than the best marksmen in the Army."

"She IS pretty good," Nan said. Jack and Caroline just watched.

Annie gave a running commentary as she showed her shooting skill. "This is my last stunt," she finally said as she walked toward Stan and Caroline's spot on the sidelines. "This is a half dollar," she said to Stan. I want you to throw it into the air as high as you can."

Stan nodded. He put the coin into his mouth and bit it to show the crowd it was real. He held it up in the air and turned it this way and that to show it was whole. Caroline was surprised to see Stan had a bit of showmanship in him, too. He wound up and threw the coin into the air as high as he could.

Pow! Pow! Pow! The coin fell to the ground and Annie jogged over to retrieve it.

She held it up to the sky and clear as anything Caroline could see three holes in the coin, Not one, not two, but three.

Annie jogged back to the sidelines and handed the coin to Jack. He took it from her while his mouth hung open. He turned the coin in his hand, from one side to another. Annie bowed right in front of him and then ran to the center of the arena where she bowed again. She ran into the back door of the blacksmith shop with her fringes wiggling.

The children clapped and clapped.

Chapter 16

Lily's head was still bent over her pot holder when Caroline returned to the table. She had one of her pigtail ends in her mouth for concentration. "Oh, there you are," she said when she noticed Caroline.

"How did it go?" Caroline asked.

"I sold three pot holders and one apron," Lily said with a smile . . . and I almost finished my mother's pot holder. She held the project up for Caroline to see. It was going together nicely and was nearly finished except for the binding. Her stitches looked to be about four to an inch. A nice standard for an eight-year-old.

Lily had put the money from her sales into a bag. She handed it over to Caroline. "Can I have the needle?" Lily asked.

Caroline didn't count the money but shoved it into her leather money pouch. "You can have the needle and the thimble for watching my table. For making three sales I'm going to give you another pot holder kit." Caroline handed the child a mostly blue kit that coordinated with the red kit Lily had chosen. "Thank you so much."

"Thank you," Lily said back. She tucked her new kit and her nearly finished kit into her backpack. "I could hear the gun shots from here," she said. "I knew you'd be back soon."

"Are you sure you're only eight?" Caroline asked.

"Well, eight and a half," the child said.

"You seem more like you are going on thirty-one."

Lily gave Caroline another smile. "My mother says that sometimes but she says forty- seven. I think grown-ups are sort of weird."

"You are unquestionably correct."

Lily skipped off toward the school house and didn't look back.

The busses had started to load when Annie stopped by the quilting tent. "What did you think of my shooting demonstration?" she asked.

"It was quite impressive," Caroline bragged. "Where did you learn to do that?"

"I started hunting with my father when I was six and I practiced and practiced till I got perfect. That's just how the real Annie learned. She practiced till she was perfect every time."

"It was very impressive and I think Jack will be sleeping with your half dollar for a while. Thank you for giving it to him."

"You're welcome," Annie said. "I'm going to stop by and tell Kenny good afternoon. I'll see you later." The woman waved after she flicked a speck of dust off her pink outfit. She headed toward the sale tent. And Caroline watched her go.

Caroline was clearing up her table and setting it inside the quilting tent when she heard the first shot and then the second and the third. She hurried outside and watched as Annie pointed her gun at Kenny and fired three more times.

"Stop," Caroline yelled at the top of her lungs. "Stop! Annie! What is wrong with you?"

Caroline ran as fast as she could toward the sale tent. Kenny was laying on the ground with his hands covering his head. Caroline knelt beside him and rolled him to his back. He was peaking at her from the slits between his eyelids. Several people from nearby tents had begun to gather. "Are you okay?" Caroline asked.

"I think so," Kenny said.

"Blanks!" Annie said. "I was shooting blanks." She holstered her gun and laughed, pointing at Kenny as he checked himself out. He was still on the ground. He was not smiling at Annie's little joke.

"He's having a psychological effect. People who think they've been shot, act like they've been shot. It happens all the time." Annie turned to the small crowd that had gathered. "It's all a joke," she said. "He's fine." She offered her hand to help him up off the ground.

He turned away from her and took Caroline's hand. She grabbed it and helped Kenny to his feet. "That wasn't the least bit funny, Annie," Caroline said to the woman in the pale pink suit.

"I thought it was hysterical," Annie said. She looked at Caroline and then turned her eyes to Kenny and stared. "Just remember I can do it for real any time I want." She turned on the toe of her cowgirl boots and walked off toward the blacksmith building.

The only people left standing outside the sale tent were Kenny, Caroline, Melissa and Clarissa. "Are you all right, Ken?" Clarissa asked. She put a hand on his arm and rubbed it.

"Should we call the police?" Caroline asked.

"I'm fine," Kenny said in a sharp tone of voice. "Just fine." He jerked his arm away from Clarissa and stalked into his tent.

Melissa took her sister by the arm and the three women walked back toward the quilting tent. "That woman is crazy." Melissa said as they walked.

There was no one to disagree.

Chapter 17

Caroline was home with her feet propped up on a kitchen chair pulled out from the table. Jamie sat across from her blowing on a very hot cup of cocoa. "My day was a mess," she said to her mother.

"Tell me about it." Caroline said with a sigh.

"I had to buy books for my class and the bookstore was a nightmare. Everyone else was buying their books, too. Mine cost over three hundred dollars, on top of the nearly five hundred we had to pay for Ted's." Jamie took a sip of her cocoa. "I may have to get a job."

Caroline sat up on her chair, let her feet drop to the floor. "Don't you think that would be spreading yourself a bit too thin?"

"Mom, Ted and I have to have an income of some kind."

"What's wrong with Ted's getting a job. He's not pregnant."

Jamie's forehead crinkled. "He will be far too busy to work until he gets settled in to his classes. Do you know how hard law school is?"

"I've never been so, no, I don't know how hard it is, but I've been pregnant and I know how hard that is."

"I feel fine," Jamie said. Then, trying to change the subject. "How was your day, Mom?"

"I decided Annie Oakley is nuts," she said. "But boy can she shoot a gun."

She described Annie's sharp-shooter act right up to her giving Jack the shot-full-of-holes half dollar.

"Sounds like really something."

"It was. And then when the show was over she stopped by my table and then went to Kenny's tent and emptied her gun into him."

"What?" Jamie said. "What did you say."

"You heard me. Everybody nearly died when the shooting started. Annie told us it was a joke. She was shooting blanks."

Jamie's eyes were wide and her hand went instinctively to her belly. Caroline couldn't help but notice.

"Life is difficult, Jamie. You may as well learn that sooner, rather than later."

Just as Caroline gave her daughter this piece of advice Budd and Nick came in the kitchen. Their cheeks were red from the outdoor air. "Could I borrow your car tomorrow?" Budd asked her mother.

"Jamie has been using it." Caroline held out an arm like Vanna White show-casing a Los Vegas vacation. "Will you be needing the car tomorrow?"

"Not if I can get Ted's cleaned out the rest of the way this evening. Maybe Budd and Nick would help me." The negotiations continued over use of Caroline's car. She was going to have to get a ride again tomorrow.

Ted and Charles came into the kitchen from the garage. They were laughing over some shared joke. Caroline stood up and began to putter in the fridge looking for something to prepare for supper. This was getting to be a routine.

Much later that night Caroline was disturbed by a noise. She crept out of her bed and hurried to the door to see what it might be. She quietly cracked the door and peeked out. There was Jamie sneaking across the hall to Ted in her old room. Caroline took a sharp intake of breath and covered her mouth. She stood by the door till Jamie closed her old bedroom door behind her. Caroline heard muffled voices and giggles. Then it fell silent again.

She pulled on her robe and went down to the couch where once again Charles was spending the night. "Charles. Charles. Wake up," she said. She pushed on Charles' shoulder. He groaned and rolled onto his back.

"What? What?"

"I just saw Jamie sneak into Ted's room."

"So?" Charles mumbled.

"I don't want them sharing a room in my house till they are married."

"So? I bet your mother wouldn't have liked it if she'd known we slept together before we got married. It didn't stop us, did it?"

"This is different, Charles. Jamie is pregnant. She's going to have a baby. A baby, Charles. Don't you get it?"

"I get it, Caroline. The damage is done. What more can happen if they spend the night together?"

"I need them to get married. They need to do this for the baby who is going to be our granddaughter."

"Grow up, Caroline. The world doesn't revolve around what you want. Or what I want. We just have to do the best we can and if we manage to find a little love or a little comfort along the way, we need to take it. Don't you get it?"

Caroline was taken aback. Tears popped out in the corner of her eyes. "What is wrong with you, Charles? I don't even know you anymore?"

"You haven't known me for years. You've been too involved with yourself and the girls to even see me or think about what might be important to me."

"Who are you?" Tears rolled down Caroline's cheeks. "What have you done with my husband?" Caroline turned her back on Charles and started to hurry toward the stairs.

Charles jumped up from the couch, wide awake. He managed to grab Caroline by the arm. He pulled her into the circle of his arm. "I love you, Caroline. I have always loved you. I don't know you any more either. I want my wife back, too. The one who loves me and talks to me. I'm tired of sleeping in that ridiculous little car with my chin on my knees. I want to come home, Caroline. But first I want you to come back from wherever you've been. Worrying about the bottom line. Putting all your energy into fabric and the people who hang out in the shop."

Caroline was sobbing loudly by this time. She pulled away from Charles and could see the wet spot her tears had left on his shoulder. He looked sad. He looked confused. She wiped her cheeks with the palms of her hands and wiped them on her pajama bottoms. She turned again to go upstairs. Standing at the top of the stairs with their arms around one another were Jamie and Ted looking down at her and Charles.

Chapter 18

Kathy already had the shop opened when Caroline got there in the morning. "You look like you had a rough night," she said.

Caroline grimaced. "Don't ask."

"Okay, I won't." She began to pack the rolling suitcase with quilting kits. "Are you going to the encampment today?"

Caroline sighed. "I suppose I will, but I have to borrow a car. Jamie is using mine today. Ted needs theirs."

"It's always something with kids, isn't it?"

"And with business. I'm thinking going to the encampment isn't the best thing I've ever done. What with Stan home and Nan all atwitter with love and Jamie and Ted living in my house all blossoming with love and babies. And Charles sleeping over on the couch. It's almost more than I can bear. Ted did fix breakfast this morning before he left to go to campus." Caroline sighed.

Aggie came in through the back door. "Sorry I'm late," she said. "I was trying to put the agenda together for the guild meeting tomorrow."

"What's your program?"

"Michael is going to teach us how to make a pumpkin roll. He's says his recipe is to die for. He also wants to discuss his new, old quilt he found at the yard sale by the side of the road."

"What do pumpkin rolls have to do with quilting?" Kathy asked.

"Nothing. But most quilters also love to cook and you can't let a professional chef go to waste. So . . . we're making pumpkin rolls. Thanksgiving will be here before you know it." Aggie smiled. "We can do whatever we want. It's our guild."

"It is your guild." Caroline said. "The ladies at the encampment have several programs they do. Yesterday Shelah offered to do one of them for our guild. Do you think your members would be interested?"

Aggie examined the ceiling. "I don't know. Michael would be disappointed if he didn't get to do his pumpkin roll demonstration." She looked straight at Caroline. "I would hate to bump him. We only allow him to do one food program a year as it is."

"Maybe you could do both," Kathy said. She had finished filling the rolling suitcase and was standing by before starting another project.

"Well, maybe." Aggie was clearing the cutting table. "I'll give Michael a call and see what he thinks. How long will the civil war ladies be available?"

"Just another week and a half," Caroline said. After that there is just one more encampment for the season. It is over in the Dayton area and a long drive for a half hour program."

"We won't get another chance until next year."

Caroline nodded. "We should try to work them in."

"I agree," Aggie said. She smiled again and the corners of her eyes crinkled and smiled right along with her lips.

Caroline asked Aggie to borrow her car to drive to the encampment and Aggie agreed. "It's hard to get into reverse so I always try parking with the nose pointed out. I think you should do that, too."

Kathy helped Caroline load up Aggie's car and Caroline set out for her day at the encampment.

Kenny was in his tent talking with Annie. She wasn't quite yelling but Caroline could tell she was upset. A bunch of ten-year-olds were milling around the tent, touching everything. Caroline waved at Kenny but he was too preoccupied to notice. Caroline hoped Annie wouldn't whip out her gun and shoot him again. It was too early in the day to get all tensed up. Caroline took a deep breath and pulled the suitcase along behind her.

Caroline invited the twins to lunch. They made their way to the mess tent among a gaggle of children who were laughing and running about. Caroline wondered how they had the energy day after day. In the distance they could hear the sound of gun shots. Caroline checked her watch and saw it was time for Annie's early show.

Melissa and Caroline ate the beans and cornbread. There is something about beans cooked in an open pot over an open fire that makes them even more delicious. Clarissa had a bag of chips and a soda.

"You need to eat something more nutritious, Sissy," Melissa said. Her voice had a breathy quality to it. Clarissa ignored her with a vengeance as she nibbled her chips.

They reminded Caroline of a thirteen-year-old girl and her mother. One was bent on control, the other on revolt.

"I'm working on your program with our guild president," Caroline said. "She already has a program scheduled but it's making pumpkin rolls. The meeting is tomorrow at four. I hope Shelah can make it?"

The twins looked at one another. Then at Caroline. "I can't make it tomorrow," Clarissa said.

"What are you doing tomorrow?" Melissa asked her.

"I have an appointment for getting my hair dyed." She looked smuggly at Melissa, who Caroline could see was on the horns of a dilemma. She wanted her sister to get her hair dyed in the worst way.

"What made you decide to finally get your hair dyed?" Melissa asked.

"I decided you were right about my looking old. Besides I think Kenny would like it."

"Are you still interested in Kenny?" Caroline asked.

"Well, yes, I am. And I'm sure he's still interested in me. He waved to me this morning as I was walking past his tent."

"Umm?" Caroline said to no one in particular. Then she turned to Melissa, "So, about the meeting tomorrow?"

"I'll ask Shelah," she said after a pause. "Maybe I can do the program with her. We'll have to emphasize civil war fabrics as that is Shelah's specialty."

"That will work for us," Caroline said. "We want to share your information with our members. It doesn't matter which part of your information you share."

"Good," Melissa said. "I'll be there and we'll hope for the best where Shelah is concerned."

The three women were finishing up their lunches when Annie sauntered by. Caroline waved and Annie walked toward them.

"How did your show go?" Caroline asked Annie.

"Big crowd," Annie said. "And of course my shooting was spot-on, as usual."

"Jack loved your show, yesterday. I think he was planning to sleep with the coin you gave him."

Annie smiled. "The kids do love that," she said.

Clarissa got up and began to leave the table. Melissa was right behind her. There was no missing the fact they were snubbing Annie in a big way. "Humpf," Annie said to their retreating backs. "They are going to be sorry for their actions," she said.

Caroline would have liked saying something to cool Annie's temper but she couldn't think of anything to say. Instead she stood, removed her trash from the table and threw it away. "See you later," she said to Annie and headed back towards the quilting tent.

Chapter 19

At the end of the day Charles came to pick Caroline up at the shop. "Everybody else was busy," he said. "I was happy to come get you." She could have refused to ride home with him, but she didn't. She squeezed herself into Charles' little sports car and decided it was more important to get home than to refuse to ride with Charles.

Jamie and Budd were in the kitchen. The girls were laughing and acting silly about nothing - like sisters can do.

"What's going on," Caroline asked as she walked through the door. Charles was close behind even though she hadn't invited him in.

"Budd and I decided to fix supper this evening. No reason you should have to do all the cooking and cleaning."

"Sounds right to me," Caroline said.

"We're not kids any more, Jamie's having a baby. She's going to be a mother." Budd was slathering butter over a split open loaf of Italian bread making garlic bread. "We're having spaghetti," she said. She was obviously pleased with herself and with her sister.

"Sit down, Caroline," Charles said. He pulled out a chair for her. "Let me pour you a glass of wine?"

Caroline sighed. "That would be wonderful," she said. Charles opened the wine, Budd slid the garlic bread into the oven and Jamie broke into a chorus of That's Amore`.

Charles handed Caroline her wine. She took a long chug and sighed again. "I could get used to this."

"This is how I remember dinner at home. I've missed it," Jamie said. "Remember how we used to play cards after supper, Mom?" She didn't wait for an answer. "I think we should do that tonight. Budd and I will be partners and you and dad can be partners."

"I bet we can beat the pants off of them these days," Budd said. She was watching the butter melt and bubble on the bread. The pungent odor of garlic was wafting from the open oven door. Budd smiled at her sister.

"We'll have to see about playing cards but I love that you are cooking dinner. I just love it," Caroline said. It was obvious she loved it as she had relaxed into the curve of the kitchen chair and was nearly through her first glass of wine. She held her glass out to Charles for a refill and he obliged her.

"What about Ted?"

"He's meeting with some of the new law students this evening and won't be home till later," Jamie said. "It will only be the four of us, just like old times."

Budd took the bread from the oven and cut it into slices as Jamie dipped up mounding plates of spaghetti, meatballs and mushrooms. She placed a plate before her mother. "You put in mushrooms, just the way I like it," Caroline said with a silly grin.

"Of course, I did. Just like you like it. Just the way you used to make it for all of us."

Caroline gulped the last of her wine and tapped her finger on the rim of her glass. Charles filled it again. Budd put two slices of garlic bread on her plate and when everyone was seated, Charles said grace.

"I can't remember the last time I had grace before a meal," Jamie said. "It feels good."

"There's no place like home," Charles said. Everybody nodded, even Caroline, and after the meal while the girls cleaned up the dishes, Charles went into the living room and got two decks of cards off of the game shelf. They were dusty.

Charles poured Caroline a fresh glass of wine and she thanked him.

"Canasta," Budd said. "Let's play canasta."

"If I remember how," Jamie said. They sat around the table and played. The girls laughed every time Charles said, "I've got a hand like a foot." It was his favorite card-playing comment and the girls had been laughing at it all their lives.

Charles kept filling Caroline's wine glass and she continued to drink getting sillier as the evening wore on. Ted came in before nine and leaned over Jamie's shoulder to check out her cards. "You've got a hand like a foot," he said. Everyone at the table stared at him. "WHAT?" he said. "My grandmother always used to say that when she played cards with me."

"Dad always says that," Budd said.

"How was your dinner?"

"Good. Seems like a nice bunch of class mates. Only two of the girls showed up, but I like both of them. The guys were all great."

"New friends," Caroline said. "Nothing like making new friends." Her voice was slurring slightly and she accidentally knocked her wine glass over onto the table. It splashed over her cards and Charles's which were laying in front of her. "I have a new friend. His name is Kenny."

"I think Mom's drunk," Jamie said.

"Who's Kenny?" Budd said.

"I think the game is over," Charles said. He was wiping droplets of wine off the cards. "I'll help you up to bed, Caroline," Charles said.

Caroline started to take his arm and then remembered. "Don't touch me," she said. "Budd will help me to bed, won't you Budd?"

Budd nodded and took her mother's arm.

"I haven't seen your mother like this since she was a teenager."

"I think she is going to regret it in the morning," Jamie said. "Thank goodness I'm pregnant and can't drink for the duration."

Charles took the damp cards to the trash can and threw them in. Budd led her mother out of the room to take her upstairs to bed. Ted and Jamie went upstairs arm in arm. No need to avoid Caroline's eyes tonight. Charles returned to the couch where he made himself as comfortable as possible.

Later, much later, he crept up the stairs and into what he still considered his bedroom. He slipped under the covers and felt the warmth from Caroline's body emanating toward him. Caroline hiccupped and rolled toward him in her sleep. He put an arm around his wife and cuddled her back into a deep sleep.

Charles was gone when the sun came up. Caroline's mouth was dry as a desert and tasted of garlic. Her head hurt and she was regretful. Drinking was not the solution to her problems. It just created more problems.

Caroline turned to Charles's side of the bed to stir his covers. They were already stirred. It appeared they had been slept on. "No!" she said. "No!"

Chapter 20

Caroline was expecting to have a busy day. She grabbed a banana on her way to the garage. She wanted to get to her car before anybody could ask to borrow it. She had a headache from all the wine Charlie made her drink last night. It had to be his fault. Right?

She arrived at the shop before anyone else. Aggie was going to be late because she was bringing the ingredients for Michael's pumpkin roll. She also had to finish up the agenda for the guild meeting and make copies of the pumpkin roll recipe for the quilters. Helping Caroline out was cutting into her free time.

Caroline puttered quietly opening the change drawer and setting up the computer for the day. She'd be happy when Nan and Stan's reunion cooled off and Nan came back to work full time. She packed the rolling suitcase with new potholder and apron kits. All the while she sipped from a bottle of water. She took the weekly receipts from the safe and totaled the first four days of the week. She sold more each day at the encampment than she had in the shop. How depressing.

Kathy came into the shop at the crack of nine o'clock. She let the door slam shut behind her. The sound rebounded between Caroline's ears. "Ssshhh," she said.

"Rough night last night?" Kathy asked with a smile. "I miss Nan," she said. "When is she going to get back on her regular schedule?"

"I'm not sure," Caroline said. She rubbed her forehead with an open palm. "Another week maybe. She and Stan need some time to get reacquainted."

"It does give me a lift to see them together. Obviously they are crazy about one another."

"When were they in the shop?"

"They were here day before yesterday," Kathy said. "Jack was with them and the new puppy."

"Must be the same day they came out to the encampment." Caroline was making out a bank deposit. "Can you believe we've made more money at the encampment with these little kits that we have in the shop."

"It's been really slow in here. Thank goodness for Aggie though or we'd not be making enough kits to keep you going over there."

"I'm going to stop by the bank on my way over this morning. I hate to let deposits pile up like this."

"I noticed you have your car today."

"Yes. I got away without anyone borrowing it this morning. Thank goodness, too, since I have to be back here early for the guild meeting. Aggie should be here about one and I'm going to try to get back by two. I need my car."

"I'll work on new kits while you're gone," Kathy said.

"Thanks," Caroline said. She went out the back door pulling it shut quietly behind her.

Caroline drove through the bank and deposited her money, then headed toward Orders Road. It was a beautiful day and if Caroline hadn't felt so bad, she might have felt really good. There were four busses in the parking area and children were running every which way. She took the rolling suitcase from the car's trunk and pulled it toward the quilting tent. She waved to Kenny as she went past his tent. He waved back at her.

She set up her table and arranged the kits. Then she opened her water bottle and took a long chug. It tasted good.

She could hear gun shots and knew Annie was doing her early demonstration.

Sales were brisk. Caroline was so busy she hardly looked up. When she did there was Jamie. "Mom, I need to borrow your car," she said.

"How did you get here?"

"Ted dropped me off. He has a job interview and I have to buy one more book. Classes start on Monday, you know."

"I have to get back to the shop by two," Caroline said. "I can't just hand over my car."

"Two? I thought you were here till four."

"Guild meeting today. It's from four till six and we have an extra program this week."

"I'll be as fast as I can." There was a note of desperation in her voice.

"Never mind, Jamie. You watch the table and I'll try to find someone who can drive me into town."

Caroline checked inside the quilting tent. Nobody was free in the middle of the afternoon. "I'm going to check with Kenny."

"Kenny? Is that your new friend?"

Caroline nodded. Then she headed for Kenny's tent. Jamie tried to see her mother's new friend but she couldn't. Caroline was in and out of Kenny's tent in a few minutes.

"He can run me into town" Caroline said. She scowled at her daughter. "Remember I need a ride home from the shop at six. And don't do this again."

The afternoon went quickly. Before Caroline knew it Kenny was standing before her with his hat in his hand. "Ready?" he asked. Caroline closed down her table and loaded up a few leftover kits. Kenny took them from her and carried them toward his van.

"I closed for the day," he said. "I thought we might have time for a cup of coffee and a Danish."

"I'm sorry," Caroline said. "The very reason I have to get back early is there is a scheduled quilt guild meeting at 4:00. I'd love to have coffee and a Danish with you, but today is not the day."

"I should have figured that out," Kenny said.

"Maybe you'd like to stay for the meeting and get a demonstration on making a pumpkin roll. Then we could have pumpkin roll and coffee."

"Sounds good to me," Kenny said. And so they went forward with that plan.

Aggie was alone in the shop. Kathy had left at her regular time. Aggie reported there were only two customers all day long. She spent the day making apron and potholder kits. She had a huge pile of kits stacked on her work table. Caroline could tell she had been working hard. Several strands of hair were sticking out from her bun here and there.

"This is Kenny," Caroline said. "He's going to stay for the guild meeting."

"Wonderful," Aggie said. "We don't get too many visitors."

Kenny tipped his hat, bowed at the waist and kissed Aggie's hand. "My pleasure to meet you, Aggie," he said.

Aggie giggled, then looked at Caroline with raised eyebrows. There was a rosy glow on her cheeks.

"I have to go upstairs and set up for the meeting," she said. "I haven't taken the time yet."

"Certainly," Caroline said. "Go ahead."

"Michael should be coming soon and I want to be ready when he gets here."

"Can I help you," Kenny asked.

Aggie covered her mouth with a hand. "Maybe," she said. "But first I think you should look around. You don't get to visit a quilt shop every day of your life."

"Maybe I could sell some of your kits next encampment season," Kenny said to Caroline. "Too bad it's so late in the season this year."

"Good idea," Caroline said. "But if business doesn't pick up we may not be here next year."

Aggie was upstairs rattling chairs around and Kenny was wandering the aisles of the shop when Michael came in the back door. He was tall and rotund in a healthy sort of way. He smiled most of the time, even when nothing was funny. This afternoon he was loaded down with pumpkin rolls wrapped in foil and the brown paper bag that held his civil war quilt. "I baked some ahead so we can taste them," he said. Michael had the fragrance of cinnamon hanging around him.

"You smell wonderful," Caroline said. "I love a man who cooks."

"It's the pumpkin rolls," Michael said. "My guild ladies are going to love them. They are simple and they are delicious."

Caroline waved Kenny over and introduced the two men. "Something smells delicious," Kenny said.

"Pumpkin rolls," Caroline told him.

"MMM," Kenny replied.

"Come upstairs with me and we'll cut one of them," Michael said. Kenny followed Michael like a hungry puppy. Caroline thought perhaps the way to a man's heart really was through his stomach.

Chapter 21

Guild members began coming into the shop. Several made small purchases on their way up to the meeting. Melissa and Shelah came in minutes before the meeting starting time. Shelah carried a bag of fabric and after they greeted Caroline, they hurried upstairs.

Caroline waited downstairs for other late comers. Michael's voice boomed from upstairs with details of the perfect pumpkin roll. The fragrance of pumpkin, cinnamon and nutmeg wafted over the upstairs railing. Caroline locked up the shop and went upstairs to get the information Shelah and Melissa were going to share and to get in on the tasting of Michael's pumpkin roll.

Kenny was sitting near the front of the room and was tasting the roll samples liberally. He looked happy.

Shelah spoke to the guild members first, and she told about the shortage of fabric for both sides during the civil war. "Every scrap of fabric was valuable. Women used old quilts and even mattresses to make into quilts for soldiers. Women who couldn't go to war helped the efforts of their soldiers by making quilts to give to soldiers to cover them while they slept. Many who died were wrapped in their quilts for burial. Not many quilts of the period remain. Women used old quilts to make cot sized quilts for the soldiers. This was their contribution to the war effort."

"Both sides of the conflict made and auctioned off quilts to raise money for the war effort," Melissa said when her part of the program started."Southern women made quilts called gun boat quilts which were sold at auctions or festivals. Southern women made enough money selling quilts to purchase three gunboats. THREE gunboats." Melissa emphasized. "That is a lot of quilts."

"In the North, the same efforts were duplicated by the Sanitary Commission, which eventually became the Red Cross. It is estimated that over 250,000 quilts were made by northern women during the four years of the civil war."

The women listened raptly and Michael made some comments about the scarcity of civil war quilts that have survived till today. Michael shared his double wedding ring quilt with the group. Shelah was entranced with his find. "I'm sure it's authentic. Not finely stitched, but definitely old."

Michael was as a rummage sale/ flea market devotee and searched for antique quilts everywhere he went. His personal collection did not have a single quilt from the civil war era. If he'd found one, he said he'd have to donate it to a museum. Michael had talked to the Historical Society and they were going to evaluate the quilt. He was dropping it off at the end of the week.

Aggie stood to bring the meeting to a close. She still had little sprigs of snow white hair popping from her bun. She looked tired after a long, hard day. "Thanks to Shelah and Melissa for their presentation about civil war quilts. Please visit their quilting display at the encampment and give yourself time to put a few stitches in the quilts they are working on."

The ladies applauded.

"Now let's all sample Michael's pumpkin roll. We have made coffee. Please help yourself." The ladies stood and began to mill around the meeting room.

Caroline tried a piece of Michael's pumpkin roll. It was delicious. She picked up a copy of the recipe that Aggie had provided. She planned to make the pumpkin roll for Thanksgiving dinner. Maybe sooner since she had so many people living with her at the moment.

MICHAEL'S PUMPKIN ROLL

Cake   Filling

Powdered sugar 1 8 oz pkg softened cream cheese
¾ C flour1 C sifted powdered sugar
1/2t baking powder6 T softened butter
½ t baking soda1 t vanilla
½ t ground cinnamon
1/2 t ground cloves
¼ t salt
3 eggs
2/3 C canned pumpkin
1 C chopped walnuts

 Heat oven to 375°F. Grease 15x10x1-inch jelly-roll pan; line with parchment or waxed paper. Grease and flour paper; set aside. Arrange clean thin, cotton kitchen towel on counter; sprinkle with powdered sugar.

Combine flour, baking powder, baking soda, cinnamon, cloves and salt in small bowl. Combine eggs and sugar in large bowl; beat until thickened. Add pumpkin; beat until well mixed. Stir in flour mixture. Spread batter evenly into prepared pan. Sprinkle with walnuts, if desired.

Bake for 13 to 15 minutes or until center springs back when lightly touched. Immediately loosen cake from edges of pan; invert onto prepared towel. Remove pan; carefully peel off paper. Roll up cake in towel while hot, starting with 10-inch side. Cool completely on wire rack.

Beat cream cheese, 1 cup powdered sugar, softened butter and vanilla in small bowl until smooth. Carefully unroll cake; remove towel. Spread cream cheese mixture over cake. Roll cake. Wrap in plastic food wrap; refrigerate at least one hour. Sprinkle with powdered sugar before serving, if desired..

Be sure to put enough powdered sugar on the towel before rolling up cake so it will not stick.

Caroline hurried to unlock the back door of the shop so the guild ladies could leave. She was still licking her lips as she went.   Kenny was right behind her. She unlocked the door and pulled it open.

There stood Charles. He smiled at Caroline. "I came to take you home," he said. His smile faded when he saw Kenny standing right behind Caroline.   Charles stepped forward toward Kenny. He extended a hand. "I'm Charles Clarkson, Caroline's husband," he said.

"Nice too meet you, Charles. Caroline is a fine woman. I've enjoyed getting to know her at the encampment."

"I bet you have."

"Charles. Kenny gave me a ride to the shop from the encampment after Jamie showed up and took my car. He did me a huge favor."

"I bet he did," Charles said. "I think he needs to watch his step."

"CHARLES! Nobody asked you to come barging in here to rescue me."

"Yes, someone did. Jamie asked me to pick you up. She was still at the book store buying supplies for school when she called. They are having their typical pre-class rush."

"It was the least she could do," Caroline said. "But as you can see, I already have a ride." She looked at Kenny, her eyes begging him to agree to drive her home. He lowered his eyelids in agreement.

Charles stepped forward and punched Kenny in the nose. Kenny stumbled backward and blood began to spurt out his nose. **"CHARLES!"** Caroline yelled. She cast a horrified glance at Charles and hurried to the checkout desk where she grabbed a roll of paper towel, tore off a large strip and handed it to Kenny. He used the towel to stem the blood flow while he held his head back.

Charles turned his back and went out the door of the shop. He called back over his shoulder. "I'll see you at home, Caroline."

"Oh, Kenny, I'm so sorry. I am so sorry." She tore off more paper towel and handed it to Kenny. "I can't imagine what got into Charles. This isn't like him. . . at all!

The guild ladies were downstairs by this time and they were helping Kenny and Caroline with Kenny's nose bleed. They were also tittering among themselves about what had happened and who was to blame. Neither Caroline nor Kenny implicated Charles who had disappeared from the doorway. If they had been paying attention, all of them would have heard Charles' car kicking up stones as he peeled out of the shop's parking area. Angry!

Kenny's nose bleed finally began to subside but after Aggie saw all the guild members out, Caroline insisted on driving him to the emergency room.

Chapter 22

Kenny's nose was packed and the bleeding had completely stopped by the time he and Caroline left the emergency room. "Could I buy you supper?" Caroline asked.

"I'd love to have supper with you, but Charles is expecting you."

"Charles can wait for me till Christmas for all I care. I still can't believe he punched you."

"He loves you Caroline. There is no doubt in my mind. Seems like he would do anything to protect you and your marriage."

"He's turned into a crazy man and I'm not impressed."

Caroline drove to Emilio's. She and Kenny took a booth in the back of the pizza shop. They talked about the encampment and Kenny's plans for the winter. They enjoyed pizza and a beer together. Kenny reached across the booth and put his large hand over Caroline's much smaller hand. He gave it a squeeze and gazed into Caroline's eyes. They reflected more than friendship.

Caroline pulled her hand from Kenny's grasp and put it in her lap. They both smiled and Kenny took himself to the restroom where he pulled the packing from his nose. The bleeding had stopped. When he returned to their booth, Caroline was paying the bill. Kenny slid into the bench on her side of the table.

The waitress brought Caroline's change and laid it on the table. Kenny fumbled with his wallet. "My treat," Caroline said. Kenny continued to fumble. "I insist," Caroline said. "it's the least I can do."

Kenny shrugged and pocketed his wallet. His arm went around her shoulders and he pulled Caroline to him. "Thank you," he said. "Thank you so much." The position and the circumstances were compromising. Caroline rubbed her thumb across Kenny's cheek. She wanted to kiss him. She really wanted to kiss him. Maybe to make up for what Charles did to him. Maybe just for herself.

They sat that way for several seconds longer. Finally Caroline returned her hands to her lap and clenched them together. "I really like you Kenny," she whispered. "But . . . even if. . . maybe because Charles is such an idiot, I love him and I want to stay married to him."Caroline licked her lips and kissed Kenny lightly on the mouth.

"I understand," Kenny said. "I kind of like him myself."

They both smiled. Kenny drove Caroline home. The house was lit up like an airport. Charles was sitting on the porch. He stood and headed toward Kenny's car. "I'm sorry, Caroline. I don't know what got into me." He bent over and waved to Kenny inside the car with a silly grin on his face.

"Give it a break, Charles," Caroline said. "You've caused enough trouble. I can't believe you punched Kenny. He was just trying to help me. Just trying to rescue me from the disregard my family seems to have for me these days."

Caroline got out of the car, hooked her arm through Charles's in a modest gesture of reconciliation and led him back toward the house. He went willingly.

Caroline was inside the house only moments when the phone rang. It was Melissa and she was breathing hard on the other end of the line. "Caroline, I left my civil war resource books on one of the tables in your meeting room. Can you bring them with you when you come to the encampment in the morning?"

"Sure," Caroline said. "I may be a little later than usual getting there but I will be there. Hopefully in my own car."

"You have some lovely ladies in your quilt guild. I hope they enjoyed our program."

"It was wonderful. I learned a lot about civil war quilts AND about the civil war."

"I'm sorry Clarissa had to miss it but just wait till you see her new hair. She looks fifteen years younger. She went out this evening to try it out on the fellows from the encampment. I sure hope Kenny likes it."

Caroline hesitated and then asked the question she'd been wanting an answer to. "What exactly is Clarissa's relationship with Kenny?"

"To tell you the truth, I'm not sure how Kenny feels about Clarissa, but I think she may be in love with him?"

"Really? I hope it doesn't lead her to having her heart broken."

"Hearts get broken all the time," Melissa said. "Besides my sister and I can both take care of ourselves if we have to. She'd just a bit shyer than I. Being widowed at such a young age has been hard on her."

"I think it would be hard for anyone."

"She isn't home yet this evening and I'm starting to get a bit worried about her. She usually doesn't stay out this late."

"Maybe her new hair is making a hit with the fellows."

Melissa laughed. There was a sharp edge to it. "Well, thanks for looking after my books, Caroline. I'll see you tomorrow."

Charles was still sitting on the couch and he seemed weary.

He seemed old.

Maybe this is why he had to leave home for a while. Maybe this is why so many men leave their homes and families. Caroline had to admit she felt like a teenager again since Charles had left. She didn't know every single thing

Kenny was going to say before he ever said it and she hadn't heard every single story in his repertoire before he told it for the twentieth time.

A change was nice.

"Can I walk you upstairs?" Charles asked.

Caroline put her hands on her hips. It was a pose she had used often when the girls were small. "No, Charles. I think I can make it." She turned and started up the stairs.

"Mom! Mom." Jamie called coming in from the kitchen. "Did you have supper?"

Caroline stopped. "Kenny and I went to Emilio's," she said. "I treated. It was the least I could do after your father punched him in the nose."

"Dad? He told us they had words."

"Yes, and then he punched Kenny in the nose."

Ted had come to stand behind Jamie. "Way to go," he said to Charles.

Both Jamie and Caroline turned his way and glared. Charles did his best not to smile.

Chapter 23

Charles was still snuggled into the couch when Caroline left home in the morning. First thing she did when she got to the shop was go upstairs to the meeting room and retrieve Melissa's civil war quilt books. She put them on top of her rolling suitcase which was only three quarters full of kits today. The guild meeting yesterday had taken away from the work day.

Kathy came in with seconds to spare before opening. "Good morning," she said. "I wasn't sure I'd make it on time this morning."

Caroline looked at the clock on the wall. "Barely," she said.

"When will Nan be back on a regular schedule?"

"Not sure," Caroline said. "Next week for sure. She and Stan deserve some time together after he has been gone so long in the middle east."

"Oh, I agree," Kathy said but it was clear from her tone she could care less. She was the center of her own world and tried to make herself the center of everyone else's.

Caroline was putting together a bank deposit for the shop. The balance was up to the point that Caroline could write the rent check for the month. Kathy was putting away fabric bolts that hadn't made it back to the shelves because of the guild meeting last night. Aggie came into the shop smiling and bustling as if it were not the first thing in the morning.

"Wasn't the guild meeting wonderful last night?" she asked Caroline. "I learned so much about civil war quilts."

"Me too," Caroline said.

"Sorry I couldn't make it," Kathy said from the front of the shop.

"I wish we had time to have Shelah and Melissa back to speak again. And wasn't Michael's pumpkin roll wonderful? I want to make several of them to share with friends at Thanksgiving. It will be here before we know it."

"Maybe we can have them back next year," Caroline said. "They will be gone in just another week. I'm so glad we got to know them. If it weren't for them our sales would be flat as a flitter for the month." She shoved the bank deposit into her purse as she spoke.

Just then the bell on the front door tinkled and a little girl and her mother came in. The girl looked familiar. Long blond hair and a sweet smile. "Mrs. Clarkson," the child said. "Remember me? Lily, from the encampment. You let me watch your table."

"Lily! Hi," Caroline said with a smile at her mother. Lily gave Caroline a hug. "Did you finish your pot holders?"

"I did," Lily said and that's why we're here. This is my mother. She's a teacher and wants to buy some kits for her students when they study the civil war. She teaches second grade and I'm in fourth."

"What a good idea," Aggie said. "Every little girl used to work at perfecting her needle working skills from the time she could hold a needle."

"Do you remember that?" Lily asked.

The women laughed, including Aggie. "Not quite," she said. "But my mother did teach me to darn socks and sew clothes for my dolls when I was a girl."

Lily nodded gravely.

"So, I need seventeen potholder kits. One for each of my girls," Lily's mother said.

"What about the boys?" Lily asked.

"I doubt we'll have any takers, but add three on just in case. Some second grade boys might like to try it."

Caroline looked at Aggie. "I think we can do that," she said. "But not today. I have all my kits packed to take to the encampment and I will need more for tomorrow. When do you need the twenty?"

"Next week would be fine. I want to cover the civil war before we break for Thanksgiving. That would give us almost a month."

"We can do that. I'll have my daughter come in to help and I'll call you when they are ready."

"Can we pick them up at the encampment?" Lily asked.

"We can arrange that," Caroline said. She and Lily shook on the deal and then Lily gave Caroline another hug. She and her mother left through the front door, the way they had come in.

"What a charming little girl," Aggie said.

"She is, isn't she?" Caroline said.

"And to think that before long you are going to have one of your very own."

Caroline and the school busses were both a bit late getting to the encampment. She waved at Kenny as she walked past his tent. He waved back. Her table was set up when Clarissa came outside to say good morning.

Her hair had been cut and tinted a soft blond shade. It curled loosely around her face and gave her a much softer look than Caroline could have imagined. It was teased and sprayed making her appear taller. "I love your hair," Caroline said.

"It does look nice, doesn't it?" Clarissa said. "I should have listened to my sister a year ago." She smiled and patted the curls beside her ears. "Do you think Kenny will like it?"

"I think anyone would like it." The busses were unloading in the parking area and children had started running from exhibit to exhibit. Clarissa dodged the children as she walked toward Kenny's tent to show him her new hair.

Clarissa had not returned when screams began coming from the blacksmith shop. Children were running away from the building, holding hands and crying. Security people were running toward the building and before long sirens could be heard in the distance.

A Buckeye Grove police car sped into the encampment, followed closely by a squad. The police car slowed almost to a crawl to avoid the children. It was nearly rear ended by the squad. When the police car came to a stop, an EMT in the ambulance jumped out and began to steer the children away from the path. Teachers hurried to get their students out of the way and Kenny helped them exit the blacksmith shop.

The emergency vehicles crept past the children and pulled behind the building. Caroline thought she should do something but she couldn't think what. She tossed a jacket over her cash box and went to find out what had happened.

Caroline walked between Kenny's tent and the blacksmith's shop. Kenny was coming toward her. "What's happening?" Caroline asked.

"No idea," Kenny said. "I'll walk with you to check it out."

They rounded the corner of the building just ahead of the emergency workers. Just in time to see Annie crumpled on the ground. She was wearing her pink outfit and her pink cowboy hat was laying beside her.

"Annie?" Caroline gasped. She ran toward the figure on the ground. Kenny was close behind her. Annie was bleeding from two dozen or more cuts on her face and arms. Several of them were still bleeding and a few had coagulated and the bleeding had stopped. Her throat was slashed and blood was pouring from that wound. Annie tried raising a feeble arm toward Caroline and Kenny. It fell back to the ground and her eyes closed.

Just then one of the EMT's stepped between Annie and Caroline blocking Caroline's way. Kenny and the EMT exchanged glances and the policeman shook his head, No. Kenny took Caroline's arm and pulled her away from the scene. This was not a good sign.

Caroline said. "Is she okay?"

"I don't think so," Kenny said.

"She raised her arm. I saw it."

"She tried, but I'd say she is anything but okay. She's lost a lot blood. It looks like she was run over by a lawn mower. She must have a thousand cuts on her."

"I wonder why she didn't just shoot whoever did this to her. Did you see her gun?" Caroline asked.

"No," he said. Kenny wrapped an arm around Caroline's shoulders, pulled her into a hug, and she began to sob.

The encampment's PA system crackled and popped. Kenny guided Caroline to his tent and had her sit. He handed her his handkerchief and she slowly began to gain control of her sobs.

A squeaky voice came over the PA. "There's been an accident and we're canceling school visits for today. This is Captain Eberhard of the Buckeye Grove police department.. We're asking teachers to get students onto their busses and return to school. There is no danger to the students but the encampment has become a crime scene. For your protection we have no choice but to call off today's visits. We will come to the school later and we'll have some questions for the students. Someone will get in touch with you to try rescheduling your visit." The system squealed sharply as it was turned off.

"They're never going to be able to reschedule," Kenny said. "It's way too late in the season."

"Do you think she's dead?"

"I sure hope not," Kenny said. "I don't think so. You saw her move her arm."

The EMT's lifted Annie onto a gurney and then into the back of the squad. Her face was not covered and they were working with some speed which gave Caroline hope for her future. Captain Eberhard was supervising. As the EMT's lifted Annie and the gurney into the back of the vehicle, he put the pink hat he picked up off the ground onto Annie's gurney.

Caroline could see spots of blood on the pink hat. The blood had turned to black that looked like ink spots on the cheerful pink hat. She took Kenny's arm and continued to cry into his hankie. The siren whined into life and the squad spun tires throwing stones as it took Annie – dead or alive- to the hospital.

Children were still climbing onto the busses. Teachers and mother and father chaperones were herding kids in that direction. The children were subdued and quiet as the sirens drifted away from the encampment. It was several minutes before the birds began to chirp again and the children began to shove and bicker their way onto the busses.

Clarissa walked up to join Kenny and Caroline. She held a hand to the back of her head. "Do you like my new hairdo, Kenny?"

"What?" Kenny said. His arm was still around Caroline and she was still sniveling into his hankie.

"I said, do you like my hair?" Kenny looked puzzled but finally focused on Clarissa's new hairdo.

"Did you change it?" he asked.

Clarissa put hands on her hips. "Yes! I've had it cut and colored and styled to the tune of $85. at the Cut 'N Curl in town. Do you like it?"

The first of the school busses pulled out of the parking area. Children's faces were pressed against the glass of the windows. They were looking every which way but mostly at Kenny and the two women.

"The EMT's just took Annie off to the hospital, Clarissa," Kenny said. "She looked dead." He turned to Caroline. "I think we should follow along to see how she is."

"Yes, I agree." Caroline said and the two started toward the parking area.

"I'll go along," Clarissa said. "Do you really think she might be dead?"

Clarissa pushed herself between Caroline and Kenny and got into the car ahead of Caroline. That put her next to Kenny when he went around the car and got in the driver's seat . It seemed important to her.

Kenny waited while the second bus pulled from the driveway to the street. Children waved from the back window.

"I left my cash box on my table," Caroline said. "I forgot all about it."

"It will be fine," Clarissa said.

"My jacket is draped over it and probably nobody will notice. Besides the children are all gone." Caroline shrugged. "Not much in it anyway. Just my change."

Clarissa snuggled in close to Kenny.

"What took you so long to get over to Kenny's tent?" Caroline asked Clarissa.

"I stopped in to talk to the blacksmith. Before we finished talking all hell broke loose and then before I knew it the cops were there." Clarissa turned to Caroline.

"What happened? Did Annie faint . . . or shoot herself in the foot?" She giggled.

"She's been cut to shreds," Caroline said. "And there is nothing in the world funny about this. I don't even know if she's alive."

"Oh." Clarissa said. She turned back to Kenny and they drove to the hospital without speaking again.

Chapter 24

Kenny pulled into the emergency parking area close behind the squad. He jumped out and came around to help Caroline out of the car. Both of them hurried toward the doors, leaving Clarissa to get out of the car on her own.

A nurse met them at the door to the emergency room. It was just swooshing closed behind the EMTs. "Are you family members?" the nurse asked.

"No," Kenny said. "We're friends . . ." the nurse shook her head . . ."and co-workers."

"Nobody but family members allowed into the emergency cubicles with patients," the nurse said.

"Is she going to be okay?" Caroline asked.

The nurse shrugged. "The doctor will talk to a family member when he knows something," the nurse said.

"I'm her sister," Clarissa said. The nurse looked closely at her as if assessing her believability. Clarissa stood firm. Caroline almost believed her and she knew better. Then the nurse pushed the button that opened the door and allowed them into the emergency department. "Cubicle twelve," she said and they were in.

"Sit here till someone comes for you. The doctors are with her now."

Kenny led the way to the seats. Caroline and Clarissa followed.

"She's not your sister," Caroline hissed when the nurse had gone back through the door.

"What difference does it make? We're here aren't we?" Clarissa said. Caroline looked at Kenny who shrugged and put his head into his hands.

They sat and waited. Finally a doctor came to face them. "I'm sorry," he said. "She didn't make it."

"She's dead?" Caroline said.

"I'm afraid so," the doctor said. "What happened and when did it happen?"

"We don't really know." Kenny said.

"She had a shooting demonstration at the Civil War Encampment south of town," Clarissa spoke up. " Every day we have children visit from local schools. It's a wonderful opportunity for them to learn history. When the children arrived, they found her out behind the back smith shop. You never heard such carrying on. Kids were screaming and running every which way." She had to stop to take a breath.

"Which one of you is the next of kin?" the doctor asked.

Caroline and Kenny looked at Clarissa and then so did the doctor. Clarissa shrugged and didn't say a word.

The doctor pushed the knob to open the door. "Here's the waiting room," he said. "I'll send the police officer out when he is finished with me. He'll have questions for you."

The doctor stood with his arms crossed in front of him while the three walked out with their heads hung like scolded puppies, even Kenny.

Chapter 25

Things had settled down a bit back at the encampment. All the EMT vehicles were gone. There were still two police cars behind the blacksmith shop. A yellow crime tape had been stretched around Annie's shooting area. Policemen were gathering evidence and talking to encampment folks who were asking questions about what had happened or who might have seen something.

"Should we go over and tell them that Annie has died," Clarissa asked. She was sandwiched in the middle of the front seat again.

"I suspect they've heard," Kenny said. "The police have radios you know, and they're collecting evidence for a murder trial."

"Oh my god. Won't that be exciting? Do you think we'll have to testify?" Clarissa said. She wrapped her arm around Kenny's and crept even closer to him. "I've never testified in court before."

"You're getting ahead of yourself," Caroline said. "Let's just go see what we can find out."

And so they did. The crowd was mostly re-enactors from the camp site and even they were beginning to lose interest and drift off in groups of two and three.

A tall lanky man Caroline had seen around the encampment but hadn't met yet came toward them. He was focused on Kenny and extended a hand to shake. Kenny reciprocated.

"Hello, Pastor Gregg," Clarissa said. The man nodded toward her and then returned his attention back to Kenny.

"How's Annie," he asked.

Kenny shook his head. "She didn't make it."

The pastor bowed his head; his lips moved in a silent prayer. When it had finished, Kenny said, "Pastor, have you met Caroline Clarkson?"

"No," the Pastor said. Then "Sorry to be meeting you under these circumstances." He reached out and shook Caroline's hand.

"Good to meet you," Caroline said.

Pastor Gregg put an arm around Kenny's shoulders and pulled him from the side of the women. They put their heads together and spoke quietly for a few minutes.

"Is he a real preacher?" Caroline asked Clarissa.

"He sure is," she said." He preaches every Sunday afternoon for the campers and the public. Whoever wants to listen. He's retired and can do whatever he wants."

Caroline nodded. A plan was forming in her head that called for a pastor.

The men walked back to the women. "Do you have any idea about Annie's family?" Kenny asked Clarissa.

"I don't," she said.

He looked to Caroline who shrugged. "I don't either."

"We have to find her next of kin before we can go forward taking care of her," Pastor Gregg said to the group.

"Won't the police take care of this?" Caroline asked.

"I'm sure they will try, the Pastor said. "But they could use our help."

"Maybe Melissa knows something." Clarissa said. She reached up and gave Kenny a peck on the cheek. She had barely headed off toward the quilting tent when Kenny rubbed her kiss off his cheek.

His brow wrinkled. "I don't know about that woman," he said. He and the Pastor headed off toward Kenny's tent and Caroline went in the other direction toward her table.

Her money box was right where she had left it, undisturbed and underneath her jacket.

Chapter 26

Caroline returned to Always in Stitches feeling shaky and unfocused. Kathy had left early and Aggie was alone and cutting kits for the encampment.

"I didn't think you'd mind," Aggie said. "I feel like a regular in here after the past weeks."

"Kathy is the least of my problems. Annie was murdered today. Cut to shreds by an unknown weapon in her demonstration field."

"What?"

"The Annie Oakley impersonator. You know she was here the day we met the women from the encampment. She is dead, cut, cut, cut and left to die."

"Oh, dear God," Aggie said. Her hands went to her cheeks and tears popped up in her eyes. "Who did it?"

"The police are working on it. Kenny, Clarissa and I went to the hospital right behind Annie. Clarissa lied like a pro, got us into the emergency room by saying she was Annie's sister."

Aggie pulled a tissue out of her pocket; dried her tears and blew her nose. "So sad," she said.

Caroline gave her a hug. That's how they were when the bell on the front door tinkled and Captain Eberhard and a patrol officer from the encampment came in. "I'm Captain Eberhard," he said. "I met you at the encampment."

"Yes," Caroline said. She stepped away from Aggie and stuck a hand out to the officer. "I remember you, from the false alarm with Annie's blanks."

"Do you have time to answer a few questions for me?"

"I guess so," Caroline said, "but I don't know anything."

"You were present when Annie's body was discovered?," Eberhard said. "I'd appreciate your cooperation."

Caroline shrugged. "Of course I'll cooperate, but don't expect too much."

The cop smiled. "I'm sure you'll do fine." The officer looked around the shop. "Is there a place we could get some privacy?"

Caroline led him to her office and pulled the door closed behind them. The office was small and it was a tight fit. Caroline sat in the only chair and the officer stood by the door.

"Tell me what you saw." He took a small notebook from his pocket and began taking notes as she spoke.

"Kenny and I tried to help, but the EMT's were there by the time we got to Annie laying on the ground."

"Did you see anybody leaving the scene?" he asked.

"Just the children," Caroline said. "They were yelling and running every which way."

Caroline answered the cop's questions and he dutifully recorded her words into his little notebook, nodding as he wrote. She even told him how easily Clarissa had lied their way into the emergency room.

When they came out of the office/closet area, Aggie was still cutting kits and stuffing them into bags. The officer thanked Caroline for her cooperation and said he might have more questions later. Caroline and Aggie watched him leave the shop by the front door, the same way he had entered.

"I'm exhausted," Caroline said to Aggie. She looked at the clock. It wasn't yet five o'clock. "I think we should close the shop and go home."

Aggie hugged Caroline. "I can tell you're finished for the day." She tossed the last kit into a box and they locked up and left.

Charlie and the Budd were in the kitchen working on supper. They were making noodles and flour was everywhere. Charlie had a belt of it across the front of his trousers where the counter top met his stomach when he leaned in. They had a mess going on. Caroline took one look and walked straight through the room to the stairs.

"Hi, Mom," Budd called. "Dad's teaching me to make noodles just like his mother used to make. "Come and see."

"Your grandmother never made a mess like that in her life." Caroline started up the stairs and didn't look back. She slept for an hour and when she got back downstairs, the mess was cleaned up, chicken and noodles were bubbling on the stove and Charlie and Budd were sitting around the kitchen table chatting with Kenny and the Reverend Gregg.

Charles stood and went to Caroline. "Are you okay?" he asked. "Kenny said there was a murder at the encampment today. The sharpshooter?"

"Annie," Caroline said.

Charles pulled her close into a hug and she allowed him to do it. It felt good.

"I think you should stay away from there," Charles said.

"Aggie's been making kits all day and the encampment is the only place I've sold a thing for over a week. I can't afford to stay away at this point." She pulled away from Charles and sat down at the table between Kenny and the preacher.. "Reverend Gregg, I wasn't expecting to see you again so soon," she said.

"Kenny asked me to come along with him. We weren't too sure how Charles would react to his visit." The preacher smiled. "Thank goodness they are getting on fine."

At just that time Jamie and Ted came into the kitchen. They were holding hands and laughing. They stopped short when they saw the group gathered around the table. "Sure smells good in here," Jamie said.

"Dad taught me how to make Grandma's noodles," Budd said.

"You'll have to teach me," Jamie said. She smiled at Ted. "Grandma's noodles are one tradition I'd like to carry into my own family."

"Speaking of family," Caroline said. "This is Pastor Gregg from the encampment. She introduced Ted and Jamie. "They are getting married."

"Congratulations," Pastor Gregg said. He reached out to shake Ted's hand. "Have you set a date yet?"

"No," Jamie said.

"Not yet," Caroline said, "but time is of the essence."

Pastor Gregg had a puzzled look that caused creases between his eyebrows.

"We're expecting a baby," Jamie said. She took Ted's hand and squeezed.

"Ah," the pastor said nodding his head. "Time is of the essence, at least for the baby's sake."

"That's what I told them. A baby should come into this world with both a mother and a father legally bound to look out for her. Don't you agree, Pastor ?"

"Actually I do agree," he said. "It's good for everyone involved to have an intact home to welcome the baby to the world."

"She's going to be the most welcome baby you've ever seen," Ted said.

"It's a girl?" the pastor said. "How wonderful. I have a daughter who is ten-years- old. I thank God for her every day of her life."

Caroline smiled and looked from Jamie and Ted to the pastor. "Maybe you could perform the ceremony." She said.

"I could," he said, "But that decision goes to the bride and groom. Then there's the marriage license and the blood tests and all the other legal stuff that has to be done."

Jamie nodded. "We know and we just haven't had time. Ted was asked to fill a vacancy at OSU law school. We had to move from Bowling Green and get prepared for him to get started. I just got my transfer today and signed up for fifteen hours so that I will only add one extra semester to my schooling. It's been a mad house."

"Surely you can find thirty minutes to get a blood test and a license." Caroline looked hopefully at her daughter who shrugged.

"Humor me," Caroline said.

"You really should," Charles said, "after all she's done for you."

"You'll never have another mother," Kenny said and Jamie said, "Thank goodness."

Charles invited Kenny and the Pastor to stay for supper; they agreed; Jamie and Ted set the table and conversation turned to Annie's murder which was much less controversial than a wedding.

Chapter 27

Nan was at the shop when Caroline arrived there in the morning. So was Aggie.

"I didn't know if you'd need my help again today," Aggie said.

Caroline glanced at Nan. "What are your plans for the day?"

"Stan is bringing Jack and Lassie about eleven and we are going to the encampment to check it out again. They do allow dogs, don't they?"

"On a leash," Caroline said.

"Stan thinks we have to help Jack deal with Annie's death. He was quite smitten with her you remember."

Caroline nodded. "Can you man the shop again this afternoon," she asked Aggie.

"I can," Aggie said, "and I can make more kits for the rest of the week."

"That's great," Caroline said. "We won't need that many more kits. This is the final week end of the encampment. They will be moving the show to Dayton before closing down for the season."

"How will that affect your friendship with Kenny?" Nan asked. She rolled her eyes as she spoke.

"I hope Kenny and I can remain friends," Caroline said. "He and Pastor Gregg had supper with us last night. Charles was perfectly polite and of course, so was Kenny. I believe this is doable."

Aggie and Nan watched Caroline with their chins sagging. They thought she might be hallucinating.

"We also discussed Ted and Jamie's wedding. Pastor Gregg may be able to perform the ceremony at the encampment. Wouldn't that be super?"

"Did Jamie agree?" Aggie asked.

"Not exactly," Caroline said, "but she's on the verge. Pastor Gregg said all they need is to find the time to have a blood test and get the license." Caroline hesitated. "She didn't say no."

"My money is on the expectant grandmother," Aggie said.

Caroline packed her car and headed off to the encampment which had become part of her morning routine.

Lily and her mother were waiting for Caroline when she arrived at the encampment. She had left the kits Lily's mother had ordered for her class and their study of the civil war back at the shop. Aggie had been working on them all week, an hour a day to have them ready for pick up today and she had forgotten to bring them with her.

"Lily, I'm so glad to see you today," Caroline said. "I've got your mother's kits ready, but I forgot to bring them with me today." Caroline smiled at Lily's mother. "Can you stop by the shop later to pick them up?"

"Of course, we can do that. We're going to take a last turn through the encampment," Lily's mother said. Lily waved good-bye to Caroline. She and her mother headed for the blacksmith shop. They were barely out of sight when Jack, Nan, Stan and Lassie walked up.

"Lots of excitement here yesterday from what I heard," Stan said.

Caroline nodded. "Poor Annie. Things have settled down. I haven't seen any policemen yet today."

Stan stuck his thumbs into the air and signaled progress. "Jack wants to search Annie's shooting area."

"We'll have to see if the tape is taken down yet," Caroline said. "I'll walk over with you to see."

"Let's check out the shooting range," Stan said.

Jack jumped up and down and so did Lily. "Will we see Annie Oakley," Jack asked shyly.

"No," Nan said. "Annie was taken to the hospital where the doctors tried saving her life. She will be at the funeral home by this time where they are no doubt getting her ready for her funeral."

The crime tape had been removed from Annie's shooting area and Lily and her mother were walking around the area. Lily waved and ran towards Caroline and her friends. "You decided to come, too?"

"I did," Caroline said. "Jack wanted to see where Annie did her shooting demonstration."

"I'm sad she is dead," Jack said.

"I am, too," Lily said. "She was very nice to me when I visited the first time I was here. Have the police caught the bad guy yet?" Lily looked from Nan to Caroline.

"I don't think so," Caroline said. "And I think she isn't to the funeral home yet. I suspect she is at the coroner's office." She addressed this to Nan.

"Oh, I bet you're right," Nan said.

Stan shifted from foot to foot. "Ixney on the funeraley" he said nodding at the children. "Small ears."

"Kids are ghoulish, Caroline said. "But okay. No more gruesome chat."

"Jack is the one who wanted to come see the scene of the crime." Nan said.

Stan shrugged. He took Jack's hand and pulled him toward the blacksmith shop. Lily followed the two of them and Nan and Lassie brought up the rear.

"Are you coming?" Nan called back over her shoulder.

"I can't leave my table," Caroline said. "You all go ahead. You can tell me all about it when you get back."

Chapter 28

Caroline straightened her table. She sold an apron kit to a seven year old girl. Melissa came out of the tent and the two of them fell into a rehash of Annie's murder.

"The police have been here all morning," Melissa said. "I think they questioned everybody before they removed the crime tape."

Did they find any clues?" Caroline asked.

"I don't think so," Melissa said. Captain Eberhard said it appeared that someone had totally cleaned up the shooting area. They didn't find even so much as a spent bullet from one of Annie's exhibitions."

"That's strange," Caroline said. "I'd think there would be some shells laying around."

"The police went over the entire area with a metal detector," Melissa said. "Clarissa has been watching them like a hawk ever since she got back from the hospital with you and Kenny. She acts like she may be trying to solve the crime herself."

"She wasn't shot," Caroline said. "Why would they care so much about the shells?"

Melissa shrugged.

"She had cuts all over her when we saw her here and at the hospital. They should be looking for a knife."

Melissa shrugged again. "Do they think it was a knife killed her?"

"I don't know," Caroline said. "But I can tell you she was pretty cut up."

Clarissa came out of the tent to get her sister. "Shelah's having a problem with two of the girls. They are bending the needles until they snap and have gone through one package since they started quilting an hour ago."

"We'll just see about that," Melissa said. She hurried into the tent to stop the foolishness.

Clarissa stood quietly kicking the dirt with the toe of her shoe. Finally she spoke. "Did Kenny say anything about my new hairdo to you last night?" she asked.

"What," Caroline said.

Clarissa repeated her question. "You know after we split up last night."

"No, Clarissa, we didn't discuss your hairdo. He and Pastor Gregg had supper at my house last night but we talked about poor Annie's death and my daughter's wedding and other things. Believe it or not your new hairdo did not come up." Caroline was shocked at Clarissa's self absorption.

Clarissa gave Caroline a long look. "To tell you the truth, I never liked Annie that well. She was always after Kenny and wouldn't leave him alone even when I asked her to."

"She won't be bothering him anymore," Caroline said and turned her attention back to her table of wares.

Clarissa smiled. "Yes, I thought of that," she said.

Chapter 29

At that very moment, Jack's puppy came running towards them from behind the blacksmith shop. Her leash was streaming out behind her. Stan was in hot pursuit and so was the rest of his little group. Lily and her mother were bringing up the rear.

Jack and Nan stopped at Caroline's table. Nan was gasping and working to get her breath. She bent at the waist and Jack patted her on the back. The rest of the crowd also stopped at Caroline's table. Only Stan kept running after the puppy.

"It's my fault," Lily said. "It's all my fault."

Nan hugged the girl. "You didn't mean for it to happen. You weren't expecting Lassie to be as strong as she is."

"It's okay," Caroline said to Lily. Then she turned to Nan. "What happened?"

"Lily was holding Lassie's leash when she pulled it lose from her hand. She ran under the fence at the back of the shooting area and ran into the tall weeds. We could see the weeds wiggling as she passed through them. She wouldn't come back even though we all were calling her."

"She's just a puppy," Jack said.

"I know. And nobody is mad at Lassie. We just have to get her back."Nan said.

"My dad will catch her," Jack said. His small chest expanded and it was obvious he thought his dad hung the moon.

As if on cue, Lassie came running their way again. Her speed was slowing and she was running in evasive circles. Stan's face was red and he was breathing hard.

Jack went down on one knee and held his arms out to the dog who ran straight into them. "Yeah," everyone yelled, including Caroline.

Lassie had something in her mouth. She dropped it on the ground and gasped for breath along with the people who had been chasing her. Stan skidded to a stop and bent at the waist like a marathon runner at the end of a long race. Slobber and dog spit was rolling from Lassie's mouth and Stan was almost in as bad a shape.

Jack hugged the puppy and she wetly licked his face. "You came back," he said and hugged the dog tight.

"What's this?" Nan said. She bent to pick up the item Lassie had dropped. Nan picked it off the ground. It was slimy and wet from being in the dog's mouth.

"Looks like a rotary cutter," Caroline said.

"Why would a rotary cutter be in the shooting area?" Nan asked.

Caroline shrugged. "There is no reason. Look, it's one of those special ones, made extra large. Especially made to cut through several layers of fabric, denim, canvas or chenille. We don't even carry these cutters in the shop. If somebody wants one we do a special order."

Nan moved the cutter from one hand to another. It was crusty and wet at the same time. Nan wiped puppy slobber onto her yellow pants where it left a dark smear. "What's that?" Lily asked.

"I think it's blood," Nan said and looked at the cutter more closely. "It could be blood." She dropped the cutter.

"Somebody call 911," Caroline said. She dumped one of her apron kits from its plastic bag. She picked up the rotary cutter with two fingers, dropped it into the bag. "This could be what killed Annie," she said.

Jack, Nan and Stan went to the bean tent for some lunch. Lily and her mother left the encampment for home. Kenny wandered over from his sales tent to see what all the excitement was about and that meant, of course, there was no getting rid of Clarissa.

It was only five minutes till Captain Eberhard peeled into the parking area. He slammed on the brakes and jumped out of the car. He hurried toward Caroline, Clarissa and Kenny. Clarissa had linked her arm through Kenny's and her head, new hairdo and all was leaning against his shoulder.

"I think we found the murder weapon," Caroline said. She held up the plastic bag.

Captain Eberhard took the bag, turned it this way and that. "You may be right," he said. "I'll take it into the lab and see what they can find out. "Where did you find it?"

"Actually the puppy found it. Stan and Nan were over walking around the shooting area when the puppy got loose and went into the tall grass. When he came out he had the cutter in his mouth and ran through the entire encampment before Stan was able to catch him. "

"What is this thing?" Eberhard asked?

It's a ---rotary cutter. It's a quilting tool on steroids," Caroline said. "It's used to cut heavy fabrics accurately. This could be used for canvass or several layers of corduroy. It isn't your normal "little old lady" quilting tool."

"Super," the officer said. "Now can someone show me where the puppy found it?"

"We'll have to get Stan. His little group is having lunch at the bean tent." Caroline tilted her head in that direction. "They'll be easy to spot. They have a puppy with them."

"I'll take you over," Kenny said. He unhooked Clarissa from his arm, smiling as he did so. He threw an arm around the officer's shoulder and they walked away from Caroline and Clarissa.

"Don't you just love Kenny's big blue eyes?" Clarissa swooned to Caroline.

"I never really noticed," Caroline said. "He's a wonderful generous man. I do know that."

"I can't believe Annie thought he might be interested in her." Clarissa straightened her pioneer dress, patted her new hairdo and followed Kenny and the cop to the bean tent.

It was a half hour before Kenny and Clarissa returned to Caroline's table. "Stan is leading the way to the shooting area. He's not sure they can find the place where Lassie latched onto the cutter, but I think they will be at it a while."

Caroline nodded. "What good luck Jack brought his puppy this morning."

"And what good luck the puppy got loose," Kenny said.

"I'm going inside to see if my sister needs any help," Clarissa said. "I'll be right back."

"Come on," Kenny said, taking Caroline's arm. "Let's go get some lunch before she comes back. She is driving me crazy this morning."

"She thinks you belong to her now that Annie is gone." Caroline said. She put her change box under the table and covered it with several apron kits and the two of them headed for the bean tent.

Clarissa didn't follow them and they had finished eating when Stan, Nan, Jack, Lassie and the officer returned. "We found the general area, but not the specific spot where the cutter was." Stan said.

"Lassie is such a good girl," Jack said and gave the dog a squeeze.

"I've got to radio the crime scene investigators," Eberhard said. "Get a team over here and see if they can find anything else."

Chapter 30

Caroline sold a single apron kit all day. There was too much other stuff going on. Nobody seemed to care about aprons when there was the aftermath of murder to deal with. She packed up early and went back to the shop.

Aggie was making more kits. She greeted Caroline and then began to hem and haw like a thirteen year old boy asking for a date. "I've been thinking," she said. "I feel good when I come in to help you in the shop. My little aches and pains fall into the back of my mind."

"Hmmm," Caroline said. She was stacking the new kits into the rolling suitcase, distracted by her task.

"I like the sense of purpose I get from coming into the shop every morning. I have always liked fabric. It is one of my favorite things. I love the feel of it; I love the look of it. I always have."

"Me, too," Caroline said. She stood up straight and stretched her back, hands on her hips and a look of pleasure on her face.

"Have you ever thought of taking on a partner?" Aggie asked and smiled shyly.

"You're eighty-three years old, Aggie. Why would you even consider taking on a burden like the shop. We haven't made $20. all summer until we started going to the encampment." She looked at the ceiling. "Well, except for when a tour bus stops. Are you crazy?"

"People have said so now and then." Aggie looked thoughtfully at the ceiling, too. "But I think they're wrong."

Caroline laughed. "I didn't mean that, Aggie. It's just that I'm not a good investment at the moment, and neither is the shop."

"I love the sounds the building makes even when there's nobody here. I love the smell of the place. The grain fragrance still hangs in the air and I especially like it first thing in the morning when I open the door. I like helping the customers when they come in with their scraps of fabric looking for just the right piece to coordinate with others. I even like it when old Robert downstairs forgets we're up here and some horrible noise comes from downstairs. This place takes me back to my girlhood. It feels like home."

"Oh Aggie, that's the nicest thing I've heard all day. I can't think about it now. I've had a horrible day. Lassie found Annie's murder weapon at the encampment and the place is crawling with police again. Clarissa is stuck to Kenny like glue and I think he's going to lose his temper with her. Lily's mother came to pick up her kits and I had forgotten them here at the shop. They got involved in finding the weapon. It never would have happened if Lassie hadn't gotten loose and run into a field of tall grass at the back of the shooting area. What a day."

"It sounds awful," Aggie said. "I had a perfectly wonderful day here. Look at all the kits I've made and I'm rested and happy. Will you at least think about taking me on as a partner?"

"I'll think about it Aggie. I promise I will, but not right now. My feet are killing me, I have a head ache and I want to go home. Can you close up the shop?"

"My pleasure," Aggie said. "You really do need a partner to help you out on the tough days and to celebrate with you on the good ones."

Caroline rolled her eyes. But the thought stayed with her while she drove home.

Jamie and Ted were in the kitchen. Jamie was cooking and Ted was sitting at the table poring over a thick book. The room smelled of Mexican spices.

"What smells so good?" Caroline said.

"I'm making taco meat. Ted liked Budd's chicken and noodles so much last night, I decided to show him what I can do in the kitchen."

"Good idea," Caroline said.

Ted looked up from his book and smiled. Hard as she tried, Caroline couldn't quite like this young man, Jamie had chosen to father Caroline's grandchild. Caroline really wanted him to hop up and give Jamie his chair. To allow her to prop her feet up. Ted should fix his own dinner. That's what Caroline really wanted but it didn't look like it was going to happen.

Charles came in through the garage. This was several days in a row he had dropped in just at supper time. Ted and Jamie's meager belongings created an obstacle course he had to maneuver through each time. He sauntered to the stove and looked over Jamie's shoulder into the sizzling taco meat. "Looks good," he said.

"You'll have to stay and have some," Jamie said. Caroline winced. It was a lot easier to weasel an invitation to dinner from the girls than it was to get her to invite him. She had to admit, but only to herself. She liked having him stop in. It seemed normal. She thought of what Aggie had said about the shop. Like home.

"What have you been up to today, Dad?" Jamie asked.

"I sold the Porsche," he said. "Got a good price, too."

"What are you driving?" Ted asked.

"My old SUV hadn't sold yet, so I bought it back. It's all nice and clean, mechanically sound and they popped out the rear fender where Budd backed into a dumpster."

"Does this mean your midlife crisis is over?" Caroline asked.

"I don't know what it means, Caroline. I do know the old car fits me so much better than the Porsche. I feel more like myself driving it."

Ted slammed his book closed and got up from the table. "I guess we're ruining your study time," Caroline said to him.

"Sort of," he answered, "but even a first year law student needs to take a break now and then."

Charles nodded his agreement and got a spoon out of the drawer. He tasted Jamie's taco mix. "Hmmm, pretty good."

"Glad I made extra so you can stay to have some with us," Jamie said.

And the doorbell rang. Ted went to answer. He came back into the kitchen with Kenny and Captain Eberhard trailing him.

"Did you find anything else in the field?" Caroline asked.

"The investigators aren't through looking yet," the cop said, "but they should be finished before dark."

"Good," Caroline said. "Then maybe the encampment will get back to normal for its last few days. I have a lot of kits left to sell."

"We – or rather they, the police – found one of Annie's relatives. He'll be here tomorrow." Kenny said.

"Good news," Caroline said. "I can't imagine being totally alone in the world."

Charles got some cheese out of the fridge and began slicing it onto a plate. Then he pulled a bag of grapes out and added them to the plate. He put the snack plate onto the counter and Kenny helped himself.

"This is turning into a party," Kenny said.

"Funerals are like that aren't they? A big celebration of survivors." Caroline said. "Tell me about Annie's survivor."

The captain spoke up. "A brother."

"A twin brother," Kenny said. "He travels with a small carnival and does shooting demonstrations dressed as . . . guess who?" Kenny hesitated giving folks time to guess. Nobody did. "Annie Oakley," Kenny said.

"You're kidding," Charles said. "A cross-dressing Annie Oakley impersonator?"

"Yep," Eberhard said. "Right on the button. He'll be here tomorrow."

"I'm surprised you found him so quickly," Caroline said.

"Computers make miracles," Eberhard said. "We found him on Ancestry.com"

"Supper's ready," Jamie looked at Kenny and the captain. "You'll stay, of course?"

"Can't say I've had a better offer," Eberhard said. And so the whole bunch of them sat at the table eating Jamie's tacos and talking about law school, survivors, and the way things go in life and in death.

The tacos were quite good and Jamie was proud.

Bedtime continued to be tense at Caroline's house. Having Charles hang around till it arrived wasn't helping much. Ted and Jamie went upstairs together. Caroline was still insisting they sleep in separate rooms. She listened for the click of two doors being closed and she heard it. Never mind Jamie would sneak over to Ted's bed in the dark of the night.

Charles was still hinting he'd like to join Caroline in their old bed. She was still saying no but allowing him to use the couch in the living room – even though he had turned in the back wrenching Porsche for a far roomier SUV.

Budd was pushing her parents by coming in later and later from her study dates with Nick.

Things were still chaotic and the passage of time wasn't helping.

Chapter 31

Caroline overslept. By the time she got downstairs, Charles was gone from the couch, Ted and Jamie had left for school and Budd was in the kitchen having coffee with lots of cream just like she liked it.

"You got in late last night," Caroline said. "I didn't hear you at all."

"It was sort of late. I was helping Nick study for a history test."

"How could he be having a test already? The semester just started."

Budd shrugged. "I don't know. All I know is we studied past regular bed time. "

"I'd appreciate it if you get home earlier in the future. Your dad was here."

"I saw him sleeping on the couch when I got in. He didn't look very comfortable." Budd took a sip of coffee. "Are you two ever going to make up?"

Caroline sighed. "I don't know. He sold the Porsche and got his old car back from the dealership. That is promising."

"What about this Kenny guy?"

"I like him, but he's just my friend. He's helped make this time at the encampment fun and I think your dad is a little bit jealous."

Caroline ate peanut butter toast. "Jack's puppy found Annie's murder weapon yesterday. Can you believe it? In the field next to her shooting area. Her brother is coming into town today. He's her lone survivor."

"Very sad." Budd got up from the table, went to the sink and rinsed her cup. "I have to get going," she said. I've already missed first period."

"Me, too," Caroline said.

The both left the family kitchen to get on with their day.

Caroline stopped at the shop. Kathy was there with Aggie. They were laughing and cutting kits. She packed up a few more completed kits and left for the encampment.

There were a dozen ten year old boys in Kenny's tent which put it pretty much at capacity. Melissa and Clarissa each came to check on her before she got her table opened up.

They were bickering, and Clarissa's new hairdo had fallen sideways. Caroline straightened the table, and re-straightened the table trying to avoid getting pulled into their morning tiff.

Out of the corner of her eye she saw a familiar figure walking toward her. "Annie?' Caroline cried and headed toward her friend Annie Oakley who she had seen dead in the hospital. Walking beside Annie was Pastor Gregg.

She was wearing a red cowgirl suit, right down to the boots and she was smiling. "This is Annie's brother, Andy," Pastor Gregg said. "I'm showing him around the encampment and he's going to collect the things from Annie's display."

"You sure do look like your sister." Caroline said.

"She would never wear red," Andy Oakley said and stuck out a hand to shake Caroline's.

"I'm so sorry for your loss," Caroline said. "We were just getting to know one another when . . . " Caroline stopped herself not knowing how to go on.

"Thank you," Andy said. "I was just telling Pastor Gregg, I think Annie would like having her funeral service here at the encampment. What do you think?"

"That's a grand idea," Caroline said. "All of Annie's friends from the encampment could come and people from Buckeye Grove who have enjoyed the encampment and especially Annie's shooting demonstrations. I think you should do it."

Pastor Gregg said, "We haven't had a funeral at an encampment since I started re-enacting. First of all we don't usually have deaths and if we do, families take their people home to be buried." He wrapped an arm around Andy and gave him a reassuring hug.

"Let's do it, then" Andy said. "I know it would make Annie happy. I might even do a shooting demonstration to send her off. That would be in the best tradition of the civil war. Lord knows there were plenty of funerals in the real camps."

"When will the police release Annie's body?" Pastor Gregg asked.

"I don't know," Andy said. "I'll find out today when I speak with Captain Eberhard."

"I'll need to do a bit of research on battlefield burials'" Pastor Gregg said.

"This will be such fun," Caroline said almost jumping up and down.

The pastor cleared his throat. Andy averted his eyes to the ground, and finally Caroline realized what she was doing. "Sorry," she said. That was totally inappropriate." So the plan was hatched to have an encampment funeral for Annie. All they needed was the body.

It was past noon when Captain Eberhard showed up. He stopped at Kenny's tent and then walked towards Caroline's table. Crime lab folks have identified the murder weapon," he said. "Thank goodness for Jack's puppy. We might never have found it in those weeds. Of course, we have all of the quilting ladies on our persons-of-interest list since it is a quilting tool. Do you know if any of the women had a grudge against Annie?"

"Not that I know of," Caroline said. "Except for Clarissa. She has an interest in Kenny."

"I can tell," the captain said. "She seems to be hanging around the poor man everywhere he goes. I've seen him give her the slip a time or two since we've been investigating this murder."

"No way this could have been an accident?" Caroline asked.

"No," Eberhard said. "You saw her. She was cut to smithereens. No way she could have done that to herself. It had to be murder. We're working at reconstructing her afternoon from six o'clock on . She was at her five pm shooting demonstration. Afterwards, she and Kenny had a cup of coffee and we haven't found anyone who saw her after that."

"So Kenny was the last one to see her alive."

"Well, no. She was still alive when the squad took her off to the hospital yesterday morning."

"You don't think Kenny had anything to do with this, do you?" Caroline asked.

"I don't know what I think yet. But it definitely was death by a thousand cuts. She must have been unconscious when she was cut to bits with the rotary cutter. Otherwise why wouldn't she just shoot her assailant?"

"Good question," Caroline said. "She could shoot the eyebrow off a gnat. I saw it with my own eyes."

Captain Eberhard went into the quilting tent when he had finished questioning Caroline. He hardly got inside when Clarissa popped out. Her hairdo had been combed out and was no longer sitting lop-sidedly on her head.

"What did he want?" she asked Caroline.

"The regular stuff. He is investigating a murder, you know. He'll have questions for each of us till they solve poor Annie's murder."

"Poor Annie, poor Annie. I'm tired of hearing about poor Annie. I think she got just what she deserved."

Caroline stopped her straightening and arranging and looked pointedly into Clarissa's face. "How can you talk that way? What did she ever do to you?"

"She interfered between Kenny and me. I think we would have been married by now if not for her. Just because she could shoot a gun. The woman was a menace. She could have shot anyone at any moment. Just because she wore those cowboy suits that were always dirty. Just because she could hit a quarter flying through the air." Clarissa stopped for breath. She crossed her arms over her chest and turned her back on Caroline. It was the closest thing to a temper tantrum, Caroline had seen since Budd was five years old.

"Calm down," Caroline said. She placed a comforting hand on Clarissa's back. Clarissa jerked her shoulder away and stomped into the quilting tent. "Wow," Caroline said. She was seeing Clarissa in a brand new light.

Clarissa was inside the tent only seconds when she came back out. She stomped off toward Kenny's tent with Captain Eberhard in hot pursuit. Melissa came out after the cop, stood at the door and watched her sister and the cop as they hurried off.

"This is a horrible end to a near perfect encampment season," Melissa said. "Poor, Clarissa. I'm not sure she will ever get over it."

Poor Clarissa?" Caroline said. "Why is she so upset anyway?"

"She never liked Annie under the best of circumstances and now that she's dead, she likes her even less." Melissa shrugged as if it was of little consequences and went back inside the quilting tent.

Chapter 32

Pastor Gregg was still showing Andy around the encampment when Clarissa headed back to the quilting tent. They met halfway. Clarissa took one look at Andy Oakley and fainted on the spot. Caroline could see her legs turn to limp noodles and refuse to hold her upright.

She hit her head when she landed on the hard packed dirt.

Caroline rushed toward them and knelt beside Clarissa. "Pastor would you get Melissa? She's in the quilting tent." He hurried off. "Do you think you could find the Captain?" she asked Andy. He hurried off in the opposite direction and by the time all had returned to Clarissa's supine body, they could hear siren's in the distance.

"I called the squad," Eberhard said. "I can hear them now."

Melissa knelt beside her sister and patted her hand. Clarissa's eyelids flickered and she began to come around. "I saw Annie," she said. "Clear as day." Her eyes fell shut again.

"I saw her, too," Melissa said. "It isn't Annie. You know she'd never wear red."

Clarissa opened her eyes again and tried to sit up. She looked around the group and rested her eyes on Andy. "This is Annie's twin brother," Pastor Gregg said. "Andy. He's an Annie Oakley impersonator, too. He's come to take care of his sister."

By this time the EMT's had arrived. They pushed everybody back, put Clarissa on a cot and hoisted her into the back of the squad. Melissa backed away from the vehicle.

"Aren't you going with her?" Caroline asked.

"No," Melissa said. "Once she settles down, she'll be fine. She's just had a shock."

"Were you friends with my sister?" Andy asked.

"Not exactly," Melissa said. "She and my sister had a little friendly competition over a man here at the re-enactment." Andy nodded as if he knew just what she was talking about.

"Where is Kenny?" Caroline asked.

"He's still in his tent with that bunch of rowdy boys," Captain Eberhard said. "I suspect he'll be over soon when he realizes Clarissa has been carted off by the EMTs."

As if on cue, Kenny came out of his tent and sauntered toward them. He was herding a couple of ten year olds in front of him. "She okay?" he asked when he got close enough.

"She had an awful shock when she saw Andy walking around," Melissa said. "He does look a lot like his sister."

"Amazing, isn't it?" Kenny said. He extended a hand in Andy's direction. "So sorry about your sister. She was quite a shot."

"Thank you," Andy said. "My father taught us both to be marksmen and it worked out well. By that I mean we both got very good at it. Something about the musculature we have. At least that's what my dad told us. Being twins and all, it worked."

"I heard you're having her funeral service here at the encampment." Kenny said.

"In front of the blacksmith's shop. That way if it rains we can move inside."

"Do you know when it will be?" Caroline asked

"Whenever the police release her body," Andy said. He looked toward Captain Eberhard who just shrugged.

"It takes longer when the police are involved and we've decided to cremate her body. So they have to really be finished with the body before we get it," Andy said with a wry smile.

"I guess so." Kenny said, but he wasn't smiling.

When it seemed there was nothing more to say, folks drifted off to their own pursuits and Caroline asked Pastor Gregg about performing Jamie and Ted's wedding.

'The request has to come from the bride and groom," the pastor said. "I know you are eager to have this done because of the baby. Marriage is an agreement between the couple and the Lord," he said. "Mother's are excluded."

"Seems to me the older the child, the more the mother is excluded in everything."

"As it should be." The pastor said. "Have Jamie call me." He headed off toward the blacksmith shop where Andy Oakley and Kenny were sharing a lively conversation.

Chapter 33

Caroline was exhausted when she got home and nobody was in the kitchen mixing up supper. She found Charlie in the living room stretched out on the couch. "Making yourself at home, I see." Caroline said.

"This is my home. I've never lived anywhere else since we moved in here when Budd was a baby. I like it here."

"What about the Porsche? I thought you enjoyed living there."

"I needed a break, Caroline. Surely you can understand that. I needed a break." His face seemed to sag and he looked old. Very old to Caroline.

"And?"

"And what?"

"What about me? What about the girls? What if we need a break?"

"I'm ready to come home. I like having Jamie and Ted here. I like seeing them every day, like it used to be. Well, except for Ted. Like the old days. With Budd popping in and out.

This is my home and I want to be in it."

"This is not a good time for me, Charlie. Surely you understand. I'm still on break." She turned her back and left him there. She went to the kitchen where she mixed up pancake batter and started sausage links sizzling in the skillet. Breakfast for supper, Charles's favorite.

Ted and Jamie were laughing and hugging as they came in. Won't they ever get enough Caroline thought to herself and then answered herself. No, they never get enough of one another and then it will be the baby they never get enough of. But never again will it ever be me they can't get enough of.

When they saw her the laughing stopped. "Did you have a good day," she asked the two of them.

"I did," Ted said. "I'm so lucky the spot opened up for me. I'm so lucky we were able to move here and step right into my spot."

Jamie smiled and hugged his arm. Her eyes said, "Isn't he wonderful, the most wonderful man who ever lived?"

She had to break it up. "I was talking to Pastor Gregg today," she said. "He's doing Annie's funeral at the encampment. He said he could do your wedding, but the two of you would have to ask him."

"I'm perfectly happy," Jamie said. "Besides we don't have time. Both of us are busy with school."

Jamie let loose of Ted's arm and her smile faded. Caroline had done her work like a pro. The mood had changed. "It's the baby who needs the wedding," she said. "It's the little one who needs to come into this world knowing both her parents and to have the protection of both." Caroline said. She flipped the pancakes in her skillet and then gave the sausages a turn. "I don't know why you don't hear what I'm saying."

"And besides if you get married at the encampment you don't need a lot of time. Twenty minutes – tops."

"She's right," Ted said. "We should just do this and make everyone happy as we are. She isn't asking that much. We love one another. We're planning to get married. Let's just do it."

Caroline might get to like this young man after all.

Jamie hugged his arm some more and they kissed. "Okay," Jamie said. "Let's just do it."

At that moment Charles walked into the kitchen. "Something smells good," he said.

"They are getting married," Caroline said. "At the encampment. Pastor Gregg is going to perform the ceremony." She left the stove and gave Charles a sincere hug. The first one he'd had in weeks.

Caroline served him up a plate of pancakes and sausage. He sat at the table and began to eat. "Yumm," he said as he chewed.

"I'll call Pastor Gregg tomorrow," Ted said. Then, "When is Annie's funeral?"

"Friday," Caroline said. "If her body is released by the police by then. But Friday is Annie's big day."

"Okay," Ted said. "We'll shoot for Saturday. In the morning?" He looked at Jamie for approval.

"Yes," she said. "In the morning. The rest of the day can be our honeymoon." They hugged and kissed to celebrate the decision. Charles munched his pancakes and Caroline released a huge sigh of relief.

The tension level in the house ratcheted down by half that evening over pancakes and sausages. Charles hoped it would help mend the rift between himself and his wife. He tried the bedroom door later that night when everyone else had gone to bed and it was still locked. His shoulders fell and he went back to the couch.

Chapter 34

Captain Eberhard was at the encampment when Caroline arrived in the morning. He had a crime scene investigator with him a trim woman with dark hair that she had swept up into a bun. Caroline thought she was beautiful and wondered why she spent her days shuffling through the stuff left by murderers and criminals.

Eberhard introduced them and Sara, her name was Sara Stone, collected finger prints from Caroline and swabbed the inside of her cheek for a DNA sample.

The cutter was crusted in blood which turned out to be Annie's and one partial fingerprint had been found. "The puppy licked the handle of the cutter and so we have lots of dog-DNA," Eberhard said. Sara laughed beautifully and Eberhard-pinked up in the cheeks. It was easy to see, he was smitten with the evidence girl.

When they had finished with Caroline, they went into the quilting tent and gathered fingerprints from the ladies. They also collected a copy of the list of women who had worked on the quilt. It was a big job.

Clarissa and Melissa came outside the tent while the Captain and Sara were still inside. They were arguing.

"I'm not giving up my finger prints," Clarissa said. "They'll be on file with the police for all time. I'll be a suspect for every horrible crime that is ever committed."

"If you refuse, Captain Eberhard will think you're guilty. Like on TV. The guy who refuses is usually the guilty one."

"I don't care," Clarissa said. "I don't want to do it."

"You'll be sorry," Melissa said. "I'm giving them mine and if they have mine they are going to have yours. We are twins, remember."

"How could I forget?"

"I gave mine," Caroline said. "It didn't hurt at all." She laughed. Melissa laughed with her but not a peep from Clarissa.

Just then the Captain and the evidence tech came out of the tent. "Thanks for the quilting list," Eberhard said. "It will be a big help in solving the crime. I have to check with the blacksmith now. Get his fingerprints and DNA." He was all business again.

"I'll walk over with you," Caroline said. My kids have decided to get married here at the encampment and I want to see if we can make the same arrangements to use the blacksmith shop in case of rain, like Andy did for Annie's funeral."

The blacksmith's name was Joe. Caroline had seen him working in the shop but they had just a nodding acquaintance. He was dressed like a blacksmith should be with a patterned shirt , western jeans and a long black apron that protected the front of his body from hot metal and sparks.

Sara did her thing with the finger print ink and the DNA swabs. Eberhard and Caroline watched. When Caroline asked about using the blacksmith shop as a back-up for Jamie's wedding, he readily agreed. It was hot in the shop and Caroline backed away from the working fire that Joe had going.

"There won't be a fire on Sunday," he said. "It does make it hot in here but the kids love it so I try to keep it going for authenticity and then of course I need it for the work I do. Look around. Make yourself at home."

Caroline did just that as the captain continued to question Joe about what he had seen the day Annie was murdered.

It was in the back of the shop, laying on a table with various tools that she saw it. "Captain," she called and

Eberhard stopped questioning Joe and walked toward her. She covered her mouth with one hand and pointed with the other. There was a large yellow rotary cutter laying amongst the tools. Its blade was not retracted and it looked like it could do serious damage to whatever it rolled over.

"A rotary cutter?" Eberhard said. "Why do you have this?" He turned and looked at Joe.

"I always keep a couple on hand. It's the best thing I've found to cut leather and my protective gear. Be careful though I keep them very sharp and you could cut yourself."

"Haven't you heard this is what was used to kill Annie?" the cop asked Joe.

"No. I have to be on alert in here with the kids running around. This is a dangerous place and I would hate for one of them to hurt himself. I don't socialize or gossip with the other folks much."

Caroline nodded to show her agreement.

"I'm going to need to take this into the lab," Eberhard said. He motioned Sara to the table and she used pliers to pick up the cutter and drop it into an evidence bag. "Do you have others?" Eberhard asked.

"I thought I had another one," Joe said. He looked but he couldn't find another cutter. "I guess not," He shrugged and looked at the captain. "If it turns up, I'll call."

"Good man," Eberhard said and led Sara and Caroline out of the blacksmith's shop.

"I'd never even heard of a rotary cutter till this week and now they are turning up everywhere," Eberhard said. Caroline smiled and headed back to her sales table. Eberhard and Stone turned toward the parking area. Their work was finished for the moment.

It was nearly noon when Charles and Jamie showed up. Charles looked handsome to Caroline. His hair was tossed by the breeze and his cheeks were a ruddy shade. Caroline's heart skipped a beat and she looked away from him. "We're here to talk to the Pastor," Jamie said. "About the wedding. Have you seen him?"

"No," Caroline said. "I've been busy with the police. They found another rotary cutter in the blacksmith shop. Can you believe it?" Then "Where's Ted? Shouldn't he be here if you're going to discuss the wedding?"

"Well...probably," Jamie said, "But he couldn't miss his class this morning and dad said he'd come with me to give me moral support – so here we are."

"I'm sure glad to see you. Kenny has his finger on what's going on around here. You should ask him if he's seen Pastor Gregg."

"We will," Charles said. Caroline pointed toward Kenny's tent and Charles and Jamie headed that way.

Business was brisk for Caroline. She sold four aprons and four potholder kits to one grandmother who was planning to give them all to her granddaughters as Christmas gifts. Ladies and children were in and out of the quilting tent and by the time Jamie and Charles returned Caroline had sold out. Melissa stopped on her way to the food tent. "It's always busy like this the last few days," she said. "People who enjoy the encampment hate to see it end. They want to get the last bit of enjoyment out of the last few days."

Whatever was going on, Caroline was happy to be doing so well. Charles helped Caroline pack up and Jamie said, "We got the wedding arrangements made. Saturday morning at 10:00 am. Pastor Gregg got word from Andy the police are releasing Annie's body so her funeral can be on Friday. He's free all day Saturday to do the wedding."

"It's a sign," Charles said. "A good sign. I'm going to give Jamie away and the lunch tent is going to serve refreshment after the ceremony. Soup beans, cornbread and pulled pork sandwiches."

"Sounds wonderful," Caroline said. "When it's over my grandbaby will have a legal mama and a legal papa and all will be right with my world."

"I doubt that," Charles said.

Caroline had the urge to brush a wisp of hair from his forehead. For the first time in a long time, Caroline wanted to comfort Charles instead of murder him. "Close enough."

"I want to wear a period costume, Mom," Jamie said. "A homespun skirt and shirt and some lace-up boots. Could you whip something up by Saturday?"

Caroline sighed. "Sure," she said. I'll look for fabric soon as I get back to the shop."

"I'll have dad take me to the shoe store to find some boots. This is going to be fun. This is going to be fine," Jamie said.

Charles and Jamie helped Caroline load up her car and they all went their own ways.

Chapter 35

Aggie helped Caroline choose fabric for Jamie's wedding dress. They decided white would be over the top and not truly symbolize purity so they went with a lovely floral print for the skirt and a pale blue cotton for the shirt. It would fit right in at the encampment.

"It's lovely for Jamie that she has a mother who sews."

"I'm not so sure," Caroline said. "I have other things to do to prepare for the wedding. Other things besides stitching up a dress for the bride."

"Like what," Aggie said. "It's a wonderful privilege to make your daughter's wedding dress. Such a personal way to be involved."

"I suppose you're right Aggie. I'm not going to complain about it. I'm the one who wants the wedding a.s.a.p. I'll make the costume and smile while I do it. I mean it's not like I haven't sewn something almost every day of my life."

"Good way to look at it," Aggie said.

Aggie helped cut pieces for the shirt and Caroline began gathering the waist of the skirt but couldn't put on the waistband when the time came. "I need to check Jamie's waist measurement. She is starting to bump out a bit." The women smiled in the way of women for all time when there was a baby on the way.

It was nearly closing time when Charles and Jamie showed up. "We found boots," Jamie said. She was excited as a child. She pulled chocolate brown lace up boots from her shoe box and showed them to Aggie and Caroline. They were a perfect match for the print her mother had chosen for the skirt. The laces and hooks went all the way up the front of the boot and they looked like they might have been made by a community cobbler in civil war times.

"I need a waistline measurement," Caroline said. She put a tape around Jamie's waist and it had expanded slightly already.

I doubt she'll need more space between now and Saturday," Caroline said. She went to the machine and sewed the waistband to size and then stitched it to the rest of the skirt. "All done, except for the handwork," she said. "I'll finish it up at home this evening."

Aggie's shirt still needed buttons added down the front. She and Jamie chose some buttons from the rack; plain white with a pearl finish and put the shirt and the buttons into Caroline's bag.

Charles and Jamie left the shop; Aggie and Caroline were left to close up.

"Have you thought about my buying into the shop?" Aggie asked.

"I really haven't, Aggie. We were busy at the encampment with the murder investigation. I found another rotary cutter in the blacksmith's shop and surely that is where the murder weapon came from."

"I know that is keeping you busy and then the wedding and all."

"Not only that, business was brisk all day. The end of the encampment rush according to Melissa. I completely sold out of kits. Lily and her mother stopped in to pick up their twenty pot holder kits and I'm flat out of everything. I don't know what I'll do tomorrow with nothing to sell."

"I put together twenty new apron kits this morning. You can sell those tomorrow."

"Thank goodness," Caroline said. "What would I do without you?"

Aggie smiled. "I was hoping you'd feel that way."

I'll let you know about the shop when the wedding is over and when the encampment moves on. I promise I will."

Caroline locked the door behind them as they left. The bag with her daughter's wedding dress was tucked under her arm.

Nobody cared about dinner that night and nobody was in the kitchen cooking something up. Budd and Nick came by so Budd could pick up study supplies and left again as quickly as they had come. Caroline sat in the living room hemming Jamie's skirt. Her head was bent over the work and she was humming. Sewing had always been therapy to her.

She heard someone come into the house from the garage. "Who's there she called but no one answered. She lay the wedding skirt aside and went to the kitchen. Charles was hanging on the refrigerator door letting cold air escape into the room.

"Charles? What are you doing?"

"Looking for something to eat. I'm hungry."

"Did Taco Heaven close its doors?"

"I'm tired of fast food. I'm tired of living without a refrigerator. I want to come home."

He looked so sad, so pathetic, so lost that Caroline almost laughed. Not with glee but from celebration. Instead she said. "Poor Charles. Let me scramble you a couple of eggs." And so she did while Charles made toast. He carried his plate into the living room where Caroline resumed her sewing while he ate.

"I can't believe Jamie is old enough to get married," he said between bites. It seems like only yesterday she was riding her bike up the street and skinning her knees and bringing home bugs."

"Hmmm." Caroline said.

"She seemed so grown up while we were talking to Pastor Gregg. She knows what she wants from life and isn't afraid to say it."

"I'm proud of her, too," Caroline said. "I just wish she'd given this baby business a little more time. A little more preparation."

"You know life doesn't always go according to plan. That's just how life is. Something new comes up and we just have to handle it. That's what Jamie and Ted are doing with the baby." He paused, took the last bite of eggs. "It's a sign to me that they can handle it. They love one another and from what I can see they trust one another, which may be the most important part. I think they will be fine and I'm looking forward to walking her down the aisle."

Caroline had finished hemming the skirt. She shook it out and sighed. "Nothing left but buttons for the blouse. I can finish that up tomorrow." She yawned. "I'm exhausted, Charles. I think I'll go to bed. Please clean up the kitchen before you leave."

"Sure will," Charles said but he had no intention of leaving. When the kitchen was clean, when the lights were turned off, he crept up the stairs and tried the door to Caroline's bedroom. It was unlocked so he went inside.

Chapter 36

It was dark and overcast on Friday morning. Annie's body had been released by the police and cremated in plenty of time to be present at the funeral. She was in an urn sitting on a make-shift alter Pastor Gregg used for his Sunday church services at the encampment. The urn was brass and had bullet shaped decorations all around it. It was engraved with a quote from the real Annie. "I ain't afraid to love a man. I ain't afraid to shoot him either." Funerals weren't what they used to be. The urn was smaller than Caroline had expected. She had started to lose friends and acquaintances at a faster clip than she had in her youth and she was learning that funerals were becoming as individual as the people who had breathed their last.

Someone had draped fringe from Annie's various costumes across the altar. It was obvious Caroline wasn't the only person who had spent yesterday in the sewing room. Someone had clipped fringe from Annie's shooting costumes and arranged them artfully around the urn. Pastor Gregg and Andy were inside the blacksmith shop talking. Andy was wearing his red Annie Oakley outfit for the ceremony.

The encampment had not been shut down and regular spectators paused by the alter and asked Caroline what was going on. The shop was closed for the morning. Aggie, Nan, Stan and Jack were with Caroline for the service. They were the core of the small crowd that was beginning to assemble. Kenny had ambled over and even Clarissa was in attendance but there was no sign of Melissa.

It was an odd little crowd.

The PA system crackled on and somewhere, someone announced that funeral services for alias Annie Oakley, the encampment's sharp shooter, would begin in five minutes outside the blacksmith shop. The announcement drew the curious and friends. By the time Pastor Gregg stood at the altar, there was a respectable crowd.

A chair had been set up next to the altar and Andy took it. He was the only seated guest. After an opening prayer, Pastor Gregg began his service.

"We know our Annie Oakley wasn't the famed shooter who traveled around the United States and Europe with the Wild West Show, but she was a show stopping shot just like that original sharp shooter.

Our Annie loved astounding her audiences and especially the children with her sharp-eyed shooting. We were all privileged to have seen her work and to have had the opportunity to know such a devoted marksman. She brought each of us a little piece of history with her performances. It is with great sadness and love that we gather here today to say good-bye.

We loathe the fact she was murdered and we cringe at the thought of who might have robbed us all of this hero for our time. We bid you fond adieu and god speed in heaven our friend Annie Oakley aka Darla Binns."

It was short and it was sweet but it was good. Pastor Gregg then introduced Andy Oakley, who eulogized his sister. His words revealed a warm regard as well as a stiff competition with his sister. "She was always the best," he said. "She practiced her shooting day and night till she was nearly perfect. She was as devoted as the real Annie Oakley. I was not.

"Our father was supervising our practice one day. – we must have been about fourteen at the time- when he told her – you are a real Annie Oakley. The name had stuck. She started using it in shooting competitions and even signed her name that way on papers for school. Sometimes I thought she really was the reincarnation of Annie Oakley. She sure could hit her target. I'm not bad myself."

Andy sat down in his chair and Pastor Gregg ended the ceremony with another prayer.

"Andy is going to honor his sister with a shooting demonstration," Pastor Gregg said. "You all are welcome to come celebrate this part of Annie's life with us. Just follow us or meet us at the shooting area behind the blacksmith's shop."

The clouds had thinned and even parted in some areas so that the sun peeked through as the folks formed a ragged parade around to the shooting area. They were not going to need to take shelter from any rain. Caroline hoped Jamie and Ted were as lucky the following day.

Andy's guns were laid out on a table and covered with an oil cloth cover. The cover was a bright red that matched Andy's outfit. Andy carried his chair and Pastor Gregg carefully carried the urn with his sister to the shooting area. Andy set the chair at the end of the table and Pastor Gregg placed the urn on the far end of the table just next to the oil cloth cover.

The crowd had picked up a few people as it moved. People took an expectant and eager breath in unison as Andy stepped to the table and pulled away the red oil cloth. The guns were arranged in sparkling order waiting for him. Two pistols and a single rifle.

Jack stayed close to his father and Nan held his hand. They stood as close to the fence as they could manage and Caroline noticed a tiny tear rolling down Jack's cheek. When the demonstration ended among much applause, Andy gave Jack a half dollar with one off-center hole in it. Andy had been honest when he told the crowd assembled for the funeral his sister was a better shot than he had ever been.

The crowd clapped politely. Caroline wasn't certain what proper etiquette required. She noticed Captain Eberhard and Kenny standing at the back of the crowd and made her way toward them. "Quite a show," she said. "I've never really thought funerals required a show, but I liked it."

"I liked it, too," Kenny said. He had a solemn expression. "I'm going to miss her."

"Even after she tried to kill you," Caroline said.

Kenny's eyebrows lifted. "She was just fooling around though she did have me going for a minute."

"What happened?" Captain Eberhard asked. Caroline described the argument and the shooting that had occurred in Kenny's tent. And the fact that Annie's gun was only loaded with blanks.

"Weird sense of humor if you ask me," the cop said. "I believe Melissa mentioned the uproar when I questioned her."

Kenny nodded.

"Are the quilters still high on the suspect list?" Caroline asked.

"Since we found the rotary cutter in the blacksmith shop I don't really know what to think. The investigation team has sent the unused rotary cutter to the crime lab to be examined. It's definitely the same kind of a cutter as the murder weapon but not the actual weapon used. We think it was stolen from the blacksmith shop and used to cut Annie up."

"I guess that puts the blacksmith on the list or moves him a bit higher if he was already there." Kenny said.

"Everybody is on our list of suspects in the beginning," the captain said. "It narrows down as we move through the investigation as we get toward the end. We'll figure it out. We almost always do."

Chapter 37

Andy Oakley hosted the funeral guests at the refreshment stand. The guests stood in small groups and chatted while Andy told stories about his sister and told of her many awards and experiences as a sharp shooter. Captain Eberhard had Sara with him again today and she was taking notes.

Caroline invited Kenny to Jamie and Ted's wedding the following day. "I hope the weather holds," Caroline said.

"It's going to be wonderful tomorrow," Kenny said. "I'm hoping to pack up my merchandise for the move to Dayton. We're opening there on Wednesday of next week. Then the season will be over."

"I'm going to miss having you all here," Caroline said. "I've done nearly all my business for the month out here. It's been a life-saver as far as my business is concerned."

Kenny smiled at her. "That's the problem with having your own business. When it's tough, it's awful. That's why I like traveling with the encampment. If business is slow in one place, I just move on to the next."

"Poor Annie. The summer didn't work out so well for her." Her eyes searched the crowd for Andy. She saw him standing by the serving table with Annie's burial urn tucked under his arm. He was in animated discussion with Clarissa. Her face was red and she was angry.

Caroline pointed Kenny's attention that way. "I wonder what that is all about."

"Clarissa has major problems. She seems shy but when she gets steamed, she's a force to be dealt with." He swiped a palm across his forehead. "Women," he said. "You just never know about them."

"She's crazy about you, you know?"

"So she says – all the time. Her sister even tells me."

"Melissa tells you Clarissa loves you?"

"She tells me how much Clarissa needs me. She tells me what a difference I could make in her life. She wants to get off the encampment merry go round and make her own quilts. That's what Melissa wants."

"Really? I thought she liked what she was doing."

"She wants someone else to look after her sister. She wants to stay home with her husband."

"The golfer?" Caroline asked.

"Yes."

"You will come to the wedding tomorrow? I won't see you again before you leave, if you don't."

"I'll be there," he said. I was even wondering if I can come and visit you and Charles during the off- season."

"What a good idea," Caroline said."We can ask Captain Eberhard to supper and behave like real grown-ups for an evening."

"Good," Kenny said. "Do you think Charles will mind."

"Charles won't mind at all. He is a happy man today." Caroline smiled a shy smile at Kenny.

"So you've mended your rift?"

"I think so," Caroline said.

"The conversation between Andy Oakley and Clarissa had gained in volume and angry tone. Melissa had joined the fray and stood beside her sister. They got so loud the rest of the crowd quieted down and turned to watch. Melissa slapped Andy Oakley right across the face and made a grab for Annie's urn. She connected on both counts. Annie's urn came out of his arms and fell to the hard dirt on the ground. It bounced twice and rolled. Andy made a grab for it and missed.

Melissa gave it a kick and it rolled in the direction of Kenny and Caroline. Clarissa gave it another angry boot. Somehow the lid popped off and as the urn rolled, Annie's ashes spread across the ground.

A horrified "Ooooh!" came from the crowd.

Melissa gave the urn another boot. It rolled again and Andy fell to his knees. Annie's ashes were strewn across the dirt-covered ground. The ashes stuck to Andy's pants and when he stood clutching the urn to his chest, itty-bitty pieces of Annie were stuck to his pants legs.

Melissa and Clarissa linked arms and walked across the open space back into the quilting tent. Both were kicking dirt as they went. Melissa looked back over her shoulder and scowled at Andy.

Kenny hurried to his tent trying to step around the ashes that were spread atop the earth. Caroline stooped being careful not to get her own self into the ashes. She brushed fragments into her left hand by shaking them loose from Andy's pants with her right. Andy stood silently with tears flowing and his shoulders bent in defeat.

Kenny hurried back to them with a whisk broom and a dust pan. He also stooped and began scooping ashes and dust into the dust pan. He tried to avoid the dust. It was tough going. Small groups slowed to watch and then moved on.

When all visible ashes were swept up, Kenny secured the lid of the urn and handed it back to Andy who nodded his thanks. "Those women are a menace," he said. "I wonder why they were so angry with my sister." His brows were knit together above damp eyes. "She's dead, what more could they want?"

"What did they say?" Caroline asked.

"They called her a tart. Can you believe it? A tart. No one was less tartish than Annie."

"I'm afraid a lot of this is my fault," Kenny said. "I dated both of them and especially Clarissa took exception to my being friends with both of them. Annie also had her moments of jealousy. It was a nightmare actually. They seemed to bring out the worst in one another."Kenny hung his head. I tried being kind to both of them but somehow it didn't work out for any of us."

"Do you think they had any part in my sister's death? Do you think they were that serious about dragging you off to Clarissa's cave."

Kenny shrugged. "I'm not worth it. I'm really not and I liked Clarissa, except when she got too clingy and I liked Annie, except when she went crazy with that gun of hers. I made a death bed promise to my wife that I'd be nice to unmarried old women after she was gone. I tried keeping it."

"Someone needs to tell Captain Eberhard about this attack on Annie. It could be a clue about who her murderer is," Caroline said.

"I'll see he hears the entire story," Kenny said. "I'm sure he has them high on his list of people of interest because of the murder weapon. I mean who else commits murder with a rotary cutter?"

"Could have been the blacksmith," Caroline said.

"It could have been anyone," Andy said. He checked the lid of Annie's urn. It was on tight,

Kenny surveyed the dusty ground. "I think we got most of her," he said.

Caroline and Andy looked, too. "Good enough," Andy said. "I think Annie would like leaving a little something behind at a place where she performed. You know part of her the-show-must-go-on attitude."

Kenny shook Andy's hand while he cradled the urn securely; like a baby. "Good to meet you, Andy," Kenny said. "So sorry for your loss. It is a loss for us, too."

Andy nodded and turning his back on the encampment walked toward the parking area.

Chapter 38

The encampment was crawling with cops again after the funeral. Kenny, Caroline and all the re-enacters were interviewed again after the discovery of the rotary cutter in the blacksmiths shop. Nobody had a moments peace. Caroline felt safer with the police present. Sara Stone returned as part of the investigative team. She interviewed Caroline again. Caroline liked the detective and thought they might become friends if the investigation lingered on.

"Who besides Clarissa might have wanted Annie dead?" she asked Caroline.

"I can't imagine being so angry with someone that I'd want them dead," Caroline said.

"It is the worst sort of thing to rob someone of his time on earth. To rob someone of his very life. No one has the right to do that to another person. I can't imagine it myself." Caroline was wistful in her answer and surprised herself as well as the detective by her answer.

"It happens all the time," Sara said.

"I know, but I can't imagine why anyone feels they have the right."

"They don't have the right but it doesn't stop some people." Sara smiled at Caroline and opened her interrogation notebook where she took notes on all of her interviews. "Tell me what you know about the blacksmith."

"He seems very nice. He is patient with the children and takes time to let some of the less rowdy little boys work in his shop." She shrugged.

"Did you notice any tension between him and Annie?"

"No, I never did. They shared space, you know. He kept to himself and didn't chum around much with the other encampment folks. His attention went to the work in the blacksmith shop."

"That's what I've heard from others," Sara said. "He doesn't seem the angry sort. I agree with you, it takes a certain level of anger to behave angrily towards other people. That's what I look for in my investigations. The angriest person is often the perpetrator of crimes."

"I don't think the blacksmith did it," Caroline said. Caroline had little else to tell her and soon the questioning was over. "Will you be here tomorrow?" Caroline asked.

"I'm not sure."

"My daughter is getting married in the morning right where Annie's funeral was today. Pastor Gregg is performing the ceremony. My husband and I are standing up with them. They haven't had time to plan a big wedding so we're doing it here to get it done."

"Big hurry?"

"Sort of. They are expecting a baby."

"Congratulations. I'll try to make it. I'll have to wait to see what tomorrow brings."

"Yes, won't we all."

Chapter 39

Caroline rolled over in her bed. No need to mess up the other half as Charles was there, snoring away. He had come into the room again last night. She liked having him there and guessed maybe they were made up. She guessed maybe he was home for good. He seemed calm again, more like the Charles she had always known. She climbed out of bed quietly, got dressed and went downstairs.

Nobody ate breakfast, though they would need energy for Jamie's wedding day. Ted had slept in his car to avoid seeing his bride this morning. Both Jamie and Caroline had insisted.

Caroline liked that they agreed on something. It had been a while. She went to her sewing room where she ironed a few invisible wrinkles from Jamie's wedding outfit and sewed on the buttons.

Jamie hurried into the room. "It's 8:30 already, mom. Are you ready?"

"I'm ready. I've been ready for two weeks, ever since I learned about my grandchild." She smiled as she spoke, turned off the iron and set it on its base to cool. She helped Jamie into the skirt and blouse. It looked good. Jamie was beautiful. She had done a good job with the outfit and with her daughter.

Charles came into the room. His hair was still damp from the shower but he was dressed and smiling. "Time to go," he said. He sang a few bars of Get Me to the Church on Time and they were out the door.

It was a beautiful fall day. Leaves still clung to the branches of trees but they were golden, red and brown. The encampment was crowded with visitors for the last week end of the session. Caroline waved at Kenny as they passed his tent on the way to the blacksmith shop. It looked like he was busy selling his wares.

There was a small knot of wedding guests in front of the blacksmith shop. Nick and Budd were talking to Nan, Stan and Jack. Caroline greeted them. "I wish it was Nan and me getting married," Stan said.

"We'll have our day," Nan said. "Maybe next year at this encampment. I do like the old time atmosphere and the casualness of the crowd."

"That would be wonderful," Caroline said. "We could make it a tradition, to have all our weddings at the encampment. It's much easier than the normal wedding that takes months to plan."

Aggie hurried up with Kathy. "We're not late are we," she asked nearly out of breath. "I had to wait for Kathy to get to the shop. We agreed to drive over together this morning."

"We're just about to start. I haven't seen Pastor Gregg or Ted yet but I'm sure they will be here soon." Charles was standing next to Caroline with his arm around Jamie's shoulders.

"You're a beautiful bride," he said to Jamie, "And I wish you every good thing in your life." She kissed her father's cheek. A tear rolled down her cheek.

"I'm so happy," she said.

Then Charles released her and bent to his knee in front of Caroline. "Will you marry me again?" he asked Caroline.

"Now? Today?" She was at a loss for words. "It's Jamie's wedding day, not mine."

"Dad already talked to Ted and me and also to Pastor Gregg. We'll have a double wedding if you agree, Mom. We want to do it."

Quiet overcame the crowd as they waited for Caroline's answer. Finally she whispered," Yes,". Charles stood and kissed her on the cheek. Then he bent her back into a Hollywood pose and kissed her full on the mouth. The small crowd erupted into applause.

The public address system crackled and screeched. A voice said, "The wedding ceremony is about to begin."

"Someone should fix that thing," Charles said. Heads nodded in agreement. Jamie and Ted stood before Pastor Gregg and exchanged their marriage vows. Their faces were solemn as they gazed into one another's eyes. After they both said "I do" and kissed a long, passionate kiss, they stepped back and Caroline and Charles stepped forward and joined hands. Charles gave Caroline a peck on the cheek before Pastor Gregg spoke. Her cheeks glowed pink.

"It's okay," Charles said to the reverend.

"We're already married," Caroline laughed. "We already have two lovely daughters."

Kenny stood to the side with Aggie and the crowd that had gathered for the exchanging of vows. People stopped all over the encampment to listen. Ted stood with an arm around his new wife's shoulders, smiling.

It was a perfect wedding and Caroline decided a happy day. Even Clarissa and Melissa had managed to get away from the quilting tent. Both of them shed a tear as the ceremony ended

"It's okay," Charles said. "We're already married." Caroline laughed. "We already have two lovely daughters."

Kenny stood to the side with Aggie and the crowd that had gathered for the exchanging of vows. People stopped around the encampment to listen. Ted stood with an arm around his new wife's shoulders, smiling.

It was a good wedding and a happy day. Even Melissa and Clarissa had managed to get away from the quilting tent. Both of the women shed a tear as the ceremony ended. All the guests made their way to the food tent in a celebratory mood.

Chapter 40

Jamie and Ted hurried home after the ceremony. Their goal was to have a few moments alone as husband and wife.

Charles drove his recycled bride to Always in Stitches and dropped her off. Kathy and Aggie were already there. They hadn't stay at the encampment for refreshments. Aggie met Caroline at the door with a generous hug. "I'm so happy you and Charles have made up. You go together better than peanut butter and jelly."

Caroline laughed. "Aggie you are the dearest person. Thank you." Caroline hugged her back.

"And here you are – a bride-," Kathy said.

"I had no idea. Seems Jamie, Ted and Charles worked it out without me. But now that it's done; It feels right."

"I feel better myself," Aggie said. "So what should we do next?" Aggie looked around the empty shop. "Too bad we don't have some customers."

Should we make up more kits?" Kathy asked.

"Last week end of the encampment," Caroline said. "Do you really think we'll be able to sell them?"

"I see a busy, crowded week end," Aggie said. "I think we should make one hundred new kits and try to sell them before the encampment moves on. Take your chances where you find them."

Caroline shrugged. "OK, why not. If we don't sell them all, we can invite a bunch of girl scouts in."

And so the three women got busy cutting kits. As soon as they had one hundred cut and stuffed into plastic bags, Caroline gathered them up and put them into the rolling suit case.

"Let me go with you," Aggie said. "I've got a few ideas I'd like to try out on the crowd."

"Your still thinking of buying the shop?" Caroline asked.

"Well yes," Aggie said.

"I promise I will think about it," Caroline said. "I've been thinking I might get some order back in my life since Charles and I remarried this morning. It means so much to know the person who is supposed to love you the most in this whole world really does love you and wants you. I feel like a huge burden has been lifted from my shoulders."

"That's wonderful news," Aggie said. "Let me give my selling techniques a try today. It's your re-wedding day. Find Charles. The two of you go off and celebrate."

We can't go home," Caroline said. "Jamie and Ted are there having their own celebration."

"You can figure something out," Aggie said. "Come on, I'll help you find Charles. He can't have gotten far.

"Try Emilio's first," Caroline said. "It's one of Charles favorite hangouts." Caroline was right. They swung into the parking lot and there sat Charles' new, old SUV amongst the cars of all the lunch crowd. Aggie drove to the front door. Caroline hopped out and with a wave, went inside.

Aggie drove on to the enactment site. Kenny helped her with the rolling suitcase. In less than fifteen minutes, she had two circles of little girls with pot holder kits hard at work. Just past noon, Aggie had to go back to Always in Stitches to pick up more kits to sell that afternoon.

She was a natural and knew she could make a success of the shop with or without the re-enactment.

Caroline took two weeks off from the shop for a honeymoon in Las Vegas. By the time she and Charles returned home, Aggie and Michael had arranged financing for the new business where they would make easy monthly payments and Aggie would be the boss. Michael built a coffee and lunch bar on the second balcony where quilters could meet, quilt and just relax. The ladies loved it and something always smelled of cinnamon and sugar.

Michael put Nan in charge of the snack bar and each day an incredible number of calories went out the door. Even the coffee bar turned a profit. Michael and Aggie began to believe they had the Midas Touch.

Michael believed it was time to liquidate his antique quilt collection and that went into the shop's bottom line. He donated his double wedding ring quilt to the Ohio Historical Society where it hangs proudly until this day. They never did solve the problem of when it was constructed but it was an item of interest in the museum.

Jamie gave birth to a perfect baby girl who weighed seven pounds, four ounces. When Caroline got the baby into her arms, she even gave Ted a hug. They named the little girl Susie Que and her butt never hit the bed unless her parents were studying.

Captain Eberhard and Sara Stone did their very best to figure out who killed alias Annie Oakley, Clarissa and Mellissa were identical twins with exactly matching DNA. But fingerprints on the rotary cutter were inconclusive. One of the twins killed Annie but nobody could figure out which one.

Clarissa finally confessed and had no sooner extended her wrists for the hand cuffs when Melissa began to sob. "I can't let you take the rap for me. I did it. I did it." She stuck her arms out in front of her for the cuffs. Blows were exchanged between the twins. Sara Stone broke up the fight. Both women were arrested and held in the Buckeye Grove Jail.

It was Sara's idea to send hair samples to the crime lab where the women's hair samples were sent to a trichologist (hair examination expert). Melissa's much bleached and dyed hair matched the hair found on the blacksmith's rotary cutter. Clarissa's hair was a dead on color match for her sister's but the hair examination left no doubt that Melissa had had possession of the rotary cutter. There was no sign of Clarissa's hair anywhere but on her head. The expert was only able to tell the hair samples apart by measuring the undyed hair on both women's heads and the sample from the rotary cutter. The crime scene hair hadn't been dyed for six weeks, the exact same time since Melissa's hair had been dyed. Clarissa's hair dye showed only two weeks' worth of hair growth.

Sara Stone figured it out by evaluating the trichology report.

"Why would you confess when you clearly did not hurt Annie?" Caroline asked when she visited Clarissa after Melissa had gone to jail.

"I owed Melissa something after all the time she spent looking after me. It just seemed right and I was the more likely suspect given my competition with Annie for Kenny's attention."

"So are you going to continue to pursue him?" Caroline asked.

Clarissa smiled. "Melissa is going to prison for five to seven years. I'm going home to her husband where I will cook, do laundry and make quilts of my own till she is released and then –" she shrugged "who knows?"

Unintended consequences do occur in life . So it was with Caroline and Charles. They announced to the family on Christmas Eve, when Susie Que was six days old, they were expecting in the spring.

Twin boys.

Finis

Mary Clark and Diana Hannon Forrester

LYNN THOMPSON is the nom de plume for a couple of quilters; Diana Hannon Forrester and Mary Clark. Mary formerly owned and operated the "real" Always in Stitches where Diana led the reading group. They decided they would move up from just reading books to writing them.

Other works from Diana Hannon Forrester

GUILD IN THE GRANARY
With Mary Clark and Jan Biggs

GLORY
A Mystery novel

TIMELESS STAR
With Mary Clark

WHERE HAVE ALL THE FLOWERS GONE?
A Memoir

ALL THE WORLD'S A STAGE
A Collection of Short Stories

www.BadgleyPublishingCompany.com